AIR MONSTER

AIR MONSTER

EDWIN GREEN

warrenbluhm.com

AIR MONSTER
By Edwin Green
Originally published in 1932
by The Goldsmith Publishing Company

This edition edited and published December 2022
by Warren Bluhm. Text is in the public domain.

Cover image © James Group Studios Inc.

Made in U.S.A.
ISBN 979-8-9863331-2-0

CONTENTS

AIR MONSTER

CHAPTER I

On Secret Duty

Lights glowed brightly in the large, bare tower room which was the headquarters of the Gerka, secret police organization of Rubania. It was midnight and a meeting of the supreme council of the Gerka at that hour could mean only the most urgent business.

Residents of Kratz, the capital of Rubania, who happened to be in the streets that night and who saw the lights in the tower of the government palace shook their heads and hurried on their way with fear in their hearts for the Gerka was the most dangerous organization in all Rubania and for that matter one of the most powerful groups of secret police in the whole world.

The creation of the new Europe which had followed the World War had resulted in the formation of Rubania, a rich, fertile land east of Prussia. It had been made a free state but Alex Reikoff, an unscrupulous dictator with a lust for world power, had risen to supreme command of the government, crushing out all opposition. He had built up the armed forces of his country until Rubania was recognized as a world power, feared for the might of its armada of submarines and the power of its fleets of airplanes, for Reikoff believed in the power of aircraft as an instrument of war.

That the midnight meeting of the Gerka was of unusual importance was borne out when Reikoff himself strode into the room and took his place at the head of the table around which a half dozen men were seated. They looked expectantly at him. Reikoff, short and dark with closely cropped hair, stroked his bristly mustache. He looked intently at the men before him. One after another met his gaze until his eyes looked into those of Serge Larko, in the uniform of a lieutenant of the air force.

"Ah, Serge," said Reikoff, "I'm glad that you could leave your beloved flying machines long enough to answer my call."

"Yes, Excellency," smiled Serge. "I came at once but there is much that remains to be done on the new XO5 before it will be ready for the long flights for which it has been designed."

"The XO5 must be ready for a six thousand mile non-stop trip by the day after tomorrow," replied Reikoff, his words short and sharp. "I shall inform the commander of your field that you are to be given every possible assistance. An emergency has come up which makes it imperative that you go soon on a special mission."

Serge, who was one of the newest members of the secret police, gasped at the news that he was to be assigned to special work. He had been trained in Germany at Friedrichshafen for service in the lighter-than-air division of the Rubanian air force and only recently had been shifted unexpectedly and without explanation to the airplane division where he had been given an intensive course in the handling of long-distance planes. For the last month he had been supervising the construction of the XO5, the latest type in Rubanian super air cruisers. Surprised though he was at the news that he had been selected for a special mission. Serge felt that he was ready for whatever task might be ordered.

The dictator of Rubania spoke again, his words cracking through the midnight stillness of the room.

"You are all well aware," he said, "that the United States is our only rival in the building of dirigibles. Their Los Angeles is antiquated now but their new Akron is superior to anything in the world. It is even a mightier fighting craft than the new Blenkko which we will launch next month. This must not be. We must be supreme in the air!"

Reikoff hammered the table with his fists to emphasize his determination and his face reddened at the thought that some nation might have men with more brains and skill than his own engineers.

"And now," he continued, "comes more bad news. The National Airways, Inc., largest passenger aviation company in the United States, has turned to dirigibles. They have been granted a large subsidy by the federal government and now have under construction an airship that will dwarf anything the world has ever known. It is intended primarily for passenger carrying, between the Atlantic and Pacific coasts, but, it is so designed that it can be turned into a powerful fighting craft, a floating mother ship in the sky that will be capable of housing a large number of fighting planes. If this dirigible, which has been named the Goliath, is completed and flies, America will remain supreme in the air for at least four more years. It would take us that long to build such a craft as their Goliath in our Blenkko aircraft plant. For America to continue supreme in the air is not in line with my plans. I do not intend that the Goliath shall rule the air."

Serge heard the last words with a sinking heart. He sensed what his mission would be. He knew now why they had rushed the XO5 to completion.

Reikoff was talking again.

"Lieutenant Larko," he said, "your mission will take you on a non-stop flight to the United States in the new XO5. Complete details will be given you later but this you must remember. On reaching the United States it is essential that you crash your plane in some manner so that identification will be impossible. You will then proceed to Bellevue where the Goliath is under construction and join the staff of the National Airways."

When the dictator paused, Serge rose to ask a question.

"But won't they question my appearance at Bellevue?"

"That will be arranged," promised Reikoff. "Before you leave Rubania you will be supplied with the credentials of a dirigible expert from the Friedrichshafen works in Germany. I warn you, however, that your mission will be dangerous. The American secret service knows that I will let nothing stand in the way of Rubania's supremacy in the air and they have been guarding this new dirigible with the greatest secrecy. Our agents in the United States have known for some months that the National Airways was building a ship to enter the transcontinental passenger service but it was only two days ago that they learned the details of the plans. Boris Dubra, one of our cleverest agents in America, has secured employment at the main assembly plant under the name of Cliff Bolton. You will work with him in the accomplishment of your mission. Completion of the Goliath will mean domination of the skies for America. It must not be."

There was a chorus of agreement from the members of the supreme council of the Gerka grouped around the table.

"The National Airways have ambitious plans for the Goliath," went on Reikoff.

"Capt. John Harkins, probably the best dirigible commander in the world, will be in charge of the big ship," he said, fingering the yellow sheets of flimsy, the wireless reports from the American branch of the Gerka which had brought news of the Goliath and its menace to Rubania's air leadership.

"Construction at Bellevue is under the direction of Charles High, vice president in charge of operations, and his son, Andy, who is reported to be an unusually resourceful young scientist and who will be Captain Harkins' first assistant."

"Your duty," went on Reikoff, addressing himself directly to Serge, "will be to win the confidence of Andy High. In America you will be known as Herman Blatz. Once you have done that you should be in a position to bring about the destruction of the Goliath. You must learn its every secret. If necessary that the ship be allowed to fly in order to accomplish that goal, do not interfere until you have mastered every secret of these American aircraft builders. When you have done that, destroy the Goliath!"

Serge nodded slowly. So this was why he had been drafted into the secret police. He was to destroy the new king of the skies. Serge loved the great, gracefully looking airships on which he had been trained at Friedrichshafen and the thought of destroying one of them sickened him. But he was a Rubanian, a member of the great army which lived as Alex Reikoff dictated and he finally forced himself to accept the mission.

The meeting of the supreme council adjourned at two o'clock and Serge drove hastily through the deserted streets of the capital until he reached the flying field where he was supervising the final work on the XO5, the new distance plane.

Mechanics were routed from their beds and set to work preparing the big monoplane for its long flight across the Atlantic. For eighteen hours Serge worked feverishly over the craft, making test flights over the field and checking every detail of the preparations. Satisfied that his craft was ready, he rolled into a bed at the field and slept for twelve hours. Awakened at dawn the second day following the secret meeting of the supreme council, he found Reikoff at the field to see him off.

Last minute instructions followed, a checking of weather maps, acceptance of the secret papers which would put him in touch with the American headquarters of the Gerka and the last words from Reikoff.

"Learn the secrets of the Goliath; then destroy that air monster."

With those words ringing in his ears. Serge climbed into the cockpit of the dull-gray low-winged monoplane, opened the throttle, shot his squat looking craft down the field and into the air. He circled the field once while gaining altitude. Then the young lieutenant of the Rubania air force headed his ship westward. He had started his 6,000 mile flight to America, a mission of destruction which was to involve the Goliath, its builders and especially Andy High, young assistant pilot.

CHAPTER II
The Air Monster

Before Andy High and the construction experts of the National Airways had arrived to supervise the building of the Goliath, Uncle Sam's newest bid for supremacy in the skies, Bellevue had been a sleepy little village in the heart of the bluegrass section of Kentucky. It had been selected as the construction site for several reasons. One of the most important was its location between two long rows of hills which insured it of protection from high winds. Another was its comparative isolation. There were no main highways leading into the bluegrass town and only one branch line railroad, which, however, was sufficient to handle the shipments of supplies.

The secrecy which shrouded the building of the Goliath was another factor in the selection of Bellevue, for the isolated little village was hard to get to without being seen and it was a comparatively easy thing to guard all entrances to the valley.

Construction headquarters had been set up almost two years before the spring in which the Goliath was scheduled for trial tests. First had come freight trains heavily laden with building materials. A little village of construction houses had gone up alongside the railroad to shelter the workmen whose task it was to build the great hangar which was to house the Goliath.

As mighty as the hangar of the Akron was, that of the Goliath was even larger. It measured 1,400 feet from one of its "orange peel" doors to the other and was broad enough for the Goliath, when completed, to nest comfortably alongside the Los Angeles, when that dirigible hopped over from Lakehurst for a friendly call.

Andy High, son of the vice president of operations of National Airways, had arrived with the first of the construction crews and had hardly left the village during the two intervening years. His father, Charles High, and Capt. John Harkins, who was to be in command of the new sky king, had shuttled back and forth between the assembly plant at Bellevue and the various factories in other cities which were supplying materials which went into the construction. It had been Andy's duty to stay on the job at Bellevue and see that every part of the carefully organized construction machine kept to its schedule for every day represented thousands of dollars to the National Airways and they made each working minute count.

The hangar had been completed and parts of the dirigible, much of which had been fabricated at the Zeppelin plant at Akron, arrived by the train-load to be assembled in the big dome-shaped shed just outside Bellevue.

On this particular spring morning, Andy was in his office just outside the hangar, pouring over the set of blueprints for the big gondola which was being assembled for the forward end of the dirigible. He was engrossed in the blueprints and failed to hear Bert Benson, who was to be chief radio operator on the Goliath, enter the room.

"Hello, Andy," said Bert quietly.

The unexpected greeting startled the young aircraft engineer and he jumped involuntarily. When he saw that his visitor was Bert he grinned sheepishly.

"Sorry I jumped like that," he said, "but we've been having so many mishaps in the last two weeks my nerves are on edge."

"I know it," replied Bert gravely. "It's been just one thing after another. First something goes wrong here and then something turns up in another part of the plant. Seems as though there was a hoodoo on this valley."

"I wouldn't exactly call it a hoodoo," said Andy, "but we've certainly been having our share of tough breaks. I'll be glad when Dad and Captain Harkins get back from Akron. Then we'll be able to give more of our time to closer supervision of the plant and these accidents may be stopped."

The words were barely out of Andy's mouth when Bert, who had been looking toward the far end of the hangar, gripped the young engineer hard.

"Look, Andy," he cried, "one of the doors at the other end of the hangar is opening!"

Andy looked in the direction Bert pointed. There was no mistake. One of the huge "orange peel" doors which sealed the ends of the hangar was swinging back on the railroad track on which it was mounted.

"Something's gone wrong down there," said Andy sharply. "A crew is working on top of that door this morning. They may be brushed off if that door isn't stopped at once."

Bert realized the danger to men working on the top of the 225 foot, 600 ton door, and he nodded grimly. There was something decidedly wrong, for specific orders had been issued that the doors were never to be opened unless Andy or Capt. Harkins were at the controls of the motors which moved the giant doors.

"Come on," cried Andy. "We've got to stop that door."

They left the office and jumped into Andy's roadster which was parked nearby. With a clashing of hastily shifted gears, they roared along the outside of the hangar. While they dashed toward the end, the door continued its slow, relentless movement. At the top they could see a half dozen men clinging to the girders. The control room for the doors was on the other side and Andy whipped his roadster around the end of the hangar. He was out of the machine before it stopped and raced toward the motor room with Bert at his heels.

There was no one at the control board and the powerful motors were humming softly. With one swift movement Andy shut off the power and the great door stopped.

"Run outside and tell that crew on top of the door to hang on for another five minutes," Andy told Bert. "Warn them to hold on tight when I start rolling the door in."

The radio operator departed on the run and Andy, looking through a window, saw Bert megaphone with his hands and shout the warning to the desperate crew clinging on top of the door.

Andy threw over the controls and turned on the motors. He let the clutch which operated the door mechanism in easily and the great "orange peel" moved slowly back into place.

While the motors sang at their task, Andy's mind was busy over this near tragedy. It could not have been an accident by the furthest stretch of the imagination for motors do not start all by themselves and clutches do not jump into place without a guiding hand. In the last two weeks there had been one minor accident after another. It had been maddening. The Goliath was scheduled to make its trial flights in two more months and there wast much remaining to be done. Each little delay meant valuable time lost and Andy had about come to the conclusion that a deliberate attempt was being made to delay the construction of the great ship. He promised himself that there would be a thorough investigation of this latest incident.

The door finally rolled into place and the half dozen men who had been in danger of their lives quickly climbed down to a place of safety.

Andy disengaged the clutch and shut off the motors. Bert returned and they made a thorough inspection of the little room but found nothing which would identify the man who had started the motors.

"Now I'll tell you why I came into your office," Bert told Andy after they had securely locked the control room. "Last night someone tampered with my radio equipment and broke up a lot of it."

Andy's lips snapped into a thin, straight line.

"How much damage was done?" he asked.

"Not as much as I first feared," replied Bert. "As luck would have it whoever used the hammer destroyed experimental equipment and the installation for the Goliath is almost intact. He must have been an amateur at the job or he would have singled out the set for the Goliath and smashed it."

"What you've told me and what's just happened," said Andy grimly, "makes me positive that there is a well-defined plot under way to injure the Goliath in every way possible. I thought we had a hand-picked crew that couldn't be bribed but it looks like I was wrong."

From the timber-covered hills behind the hangar came the sharp crackle of rifle fire, which was followed by a tense quiet as every man in the great hangar stopped work. When the rifle fire was not repeated, the crews slowly resumed their work and Andy and Bert headed for the hills on the run.

Since the Goliath had been partially financed by a government appropriation and its construction embodied secrets valuable to the war department, a military guard had patrolled the construction site from the day the hangar had been completed and the actual assembly of the dirigible started. On a number of occasions they had apprehended men trying to make their way into Bellevue and without exception the secret service detail at the hangar had found them to be agents of foreign governments. They had been quietly sent to military prisons but in the last few weeks there had been no such arrests and the vigilance of the guards had been relaxed somewhat.

Andy and Bert were half-way up the slope to the guard line when they met Merritt Timms, chief of the secret service unit at Bellevue, coming down the hill.

"Anybody hurt at the hangar?" asked Timms anxiously.

"No," replied Andy. "We stopped the door in time. What happened on top of the hill?"

"The guard had to stop a man who was trying to get away," explained Timms. "I've been suspecting one of the motor mechanics for some time of sabotage and only ten minutes ago saw him sneak out of the control room door. A second later one of the doors started to open and I knew what he had been up to. I saw you coming to shut off the power and I took after this fellow. He knew he'd have to make a quick get-away and he tried to get past the guard line."

"Did he refuse to stop?" asked Bert.

"Not only that," replied the secret service chief, "but he attempted to shoot and the guard fired, but he wasn't seriously wounded."

"I can't feel very sorry for him," said Andy, "when I think of the half dozen men, on top of the door, he almost killed. If the door had run to the end of its track with the power still on it would have ripped away from its fastenings and perhaps have crushed an end of the hangar."

"Which is exactly what this chap wanted," added Timms. "I've got a little leather packet here in which he carried some secret papers. We'll have a look at them."

The name on the leather folder was that of Cliff Bolton, a common enough American name, but the secret service man and Andy and Bert were in for a surprise when they examined the contents. Documents there showed the true name of the spy to have been Boris Dubra, an agent of the dreaded Rubanian Gerka, whose reputation for unscrupulous methods was known even in Bellevue.

"This puts a new angle on the whole case," said Timms gravely. "Of course you know that Alex Reikoff, dictator of Rubania, is determined that his air force shall be the most powerful in the world. Until just now we hadn't discovered a single Rubanian agent trying to get through the lines but it certainly looks as though Reikoff is definitely interested in the Goliath, all of which means we will have to redouble our vigilance."

"But why should Reikoff have designs against the Goliath?" asked Bert.

"It's a long story," replied the secret service chief, "but to boil it down it means that he plans to make Rubania a world power through the development of a great air force. When his planes and dirigibles are the peer of anything else in the world, he will strike out for world power."

"Which would mean another war," said Andy quietly.

"Just exactly," replied Timms, "and when the Goliath is completed and in the air it will dwarf even the great dirigibles Reikoff has turned out at his Blenkko plant in Rubania. Now you understand why the Rubanian secret police, or Gerka as it is better known, is interested in the Goliath. So far we've been pretty successful in checking sabotage and this mechanic was the only man they could get into the plant."

"He was enough," said Andy, "for had his plan succeeded and the door have crushed an end of the hangar we might have been delayed for months."

They walked slowly back toward the hangar, discussing further the events which had just taken place and planning for the tightening of the guard lines around the plant.

"As soon as this agent of the Gerka is patched up in the hospital I'll go over and give him a thorough grilling," said Timms as they reached the hangar.

"Let me know when you go," said Andy. "I'd like to see what he has to say."

"I'll do that," promised the secret service agent as Andy and Bert got into the young engineer's roadster.

When they reached the little building which served as Andy's office, they found a messenger boy with a telegram for Andy.

"Must be from Dad," he said as he ripped open the envelope, "and believe me I'll be glad to have him back here in charge of things."

Andy scanned the telegram; then he read it again hardly able to believe the words which were typed on the yellow sheet.

"What's the matter?" asked Bert anxiously.

"Nothing wrong," grinned Andy, "but it's news, big news!" With eyes aglow and face reflecting his own enthusiasm he handed the telegram to Bert.

"Rush work with all possible speed," said the message. "Have just completed plans for Goliath's first official flight this summer which will take us to North pole for an exchange of mail with the Submarine Neptune, which will be commanded by Gilbert Mathews."

"My gosh," exclaimed Bert, "a trip to the North pole. Well, that is news."

"I'll say," replied Andy. "Watch us make time from now on for there won't be any more accidents with this Rubanian secret agent out of the way."

CHAPTER III
Mystery Plane

The change of the seasons was at hand and the last dirty patches of snow melted under the rays of the March sun. Andy spread the news that the first official flight of the Goliath would take it into the polar regions and the crews inside the lofty hangar were filled with new enthusiasm and energy. They were making history, placing America in the forefront of the air-minded nations, and they thrilled at their task.

In the afternoon Andy helped Bert check over the damage which the agent of the Gerka had done to the radio apparatus and they were greatly relieved to find that the set intended for installation on the Goliath worked perfectly.

When Andy returned to his office, Bert accompanied him and they discussed the outlook for the polar flight.

"It will be a real test of the Goliath," said Andy, "and it means we'll make plenty of trial flights before we undertake a cruise into the northland."

"Why do you suppose your father decided on such a daring trip?" asked Bert.

"There has been some criticism of the government for appropriating a part of the money necessary for the construction of the Goliath," explained Andy. "This was especially true when it became known that the dirigible would eventually be used for transcontinental passenger traffic. What most people do not realize is that the Goliath will be a veritable airship of the skies, a craft that can be turned from a peace-time airship into an aerial battleship if the United States is ever attacked by an enemy force. With its enormous cruising radius of 15,000 miles without refueling it will be able to scout far from our own shores and uncover the approach of any enemy fleet."

"Then the whole idea of the polar flight will be to popularize the Goliath with the general public," said Bert.

"I expect that's about how Dad's figured it," agreed Andy. "The trial flights will take us to a good many cities in various sections and as soon as people get a glimpse of the Goliath they'll be glad Uncle Sam appropriated funds to help build it. Once they've seen the airship they'll follow its polar flight with double interest and when the Goliath comes back from the north it will be a familiar name to everyone in the country."

"Sounds like a good idea," nodded Bert. "This country needs to be air-minded or foreign nations like Rubania, which have dictators ambitious to extend their powers, will put us on a shelf."

The afternoon mail arrived and with it was a letter addressed to Andy and from the war department.

"Wonder what's up now?" he mused as he silt open the envelope. He read the letter carefully for the war department communications were usually lengthy affairs which required careful scrutiny.

"We're going to have company," Andy told Bert when he finished. "The war department has granted permission for a dirigible expert from the Friedrichshafen works in Germany to come down here and study the general plans for the Goliath. He will probably remain until after the trial flights have been completed."

"How about our construction secrets we've been guarding so closely?" asked Bert. "It doesn't seem right that we should let this fellow have the run of the works."

"We won't exactly do that," explained Andy, "for this letter outlines definitely just what information to which the Friedrichshafen man is to have access. Our own research department has had much help and advice from Dr. Hugo Eckener and his co-workers in Germany and it is only fair that we return the favor as long as we do not divulge any of the military secrets of the Goliath."

"Wonder what kind of a fellow he'll be?" asked Bert.

"You know as much about him as I do," replied Andy. "Except that I have been told his name is Herman Blatz."

"That sounds like a brand of near beer," grinned Bert. "Wonder if he'll be able to talk much English?"

"I expect so," nodded Andy. "Those chaps at the Friedrichshafen works are cosmopolitan; they have to be the way the Graf Zeppelin has been hopping from one hemisphere to another. A fellow certainly has to hand it to Doctor Eckener for his work in proving how capable lighter-than-air craft can be."

"When will this expert from Germany arrive?" Bert wanted to know.

"This letter doesn't give an exact date, but I should imagine it would be within the week. I'll show it to Merritt Timms so he won't have his secret service men chasing Blatz out of here when he tries to get through the guard line."

Bert stepped to the door of Andy's small office and scanned the clear afternoon sky. He sniffed at the air eagerly. There was no mistaking it. There was a real tang and zest of spring on the breeze. Beyond the great doors of the home of the Goliath stretched a meadow which had been turned into an airport for the aviation experts who made visits to Bellevue usually came in their own plane and ships of the National Airways dropped down several times a day.

"It's a wonderful afternoon," said Bert suggestively.

Andy left his desk with its blue prints and stepped to the door. He chuckled as he looked at the sky and then at the wind sock on the beacon tower.

"That wasn't, by any chance, a hint that it would be a nice afternoon for a little vacation in the clouds?" he grinned.

"Take it that way if you want to," chuckled Bert. "There's nothing that would suit me better than a hop over the hills. I've been on the ground for nearly a month; it's been slushy and muddy underfoot and I'd like nothing better than a joy hop."

"Tell you what," said Andy. "I feel the same way about it but I've got to check over the final specifications on the assembly of the control room in the gondola. I'm about half through now. It will take half an hour to finish the job. As soon as I'm done I'll meet you down on the field and we'll take a ride in my sportster. The sunset this afternoon is going to be grand."

"I'll be waiting," promised Bert and he left Andy alone to study over the intricate set of blueprints. Final assembly of the main control room was to start the next day and Andy wanted to be sure that he had every detail in mind. In the absence of Captain Harkins this task would require his closest personal supervision and the son of the vice president in charge of operations for the National Airways concentrated on his task before him.

Andy was a natural airman. He had first flown a plane at fifteen and at eighteen had qualified for a transport license, which he had never had time to use for from that time on he had devoted his attention to dirigibles. A year at Friedrichshafen under Doctor Hugo Eckener had given him a firm foundation for his later experiments in his father's own laboratory and he had watched the building of the Akron at the Goodyear-Zeppelin plant in Ohio. When the National Airways had decided to go into the dirigible field and construct the Goliath, suitable for passenger service in peace time or as a battleship of the skies in time of war, Andy had been given an important role in the construction program. His technical advice was sound, based on his thorough schooling at Friedrichshafen and Akron, and his more advanced ideas were supported by the experiments he had made in his father's laboratory.

Plans for the Goliath had been worked out by Charles High, Andy's father, Captain Harkins, the chief engineer and pilot, and a special board of army experts designated by the war department. If the Goliath lived up to the expectations of its builders, more ships of the same type would be constructed in the Kentucky hills while the aircraft plant at Akron was enlarged to handle the construction of other ships the size of the Goliath. Secret plans of the National Airways and the war department called for the eventual construction of ten of the giant sky liners, five of them at the Bellevue plant of the National Airways and the rest at the Goodyear-Zeppelin factory at Akron.

Andy completed his minute study of the blueprints and straightened up. He was six feet one tall, with broad shoulders and a well-developed body that revealed his love for sports in his hours away from his work. His eyes were a clear, bright blue and his light hair had just a tinge of red, an indication of his temper when he was aroused to a fighting pitch.

The sun had dropped behind the arched roof of the main hangar when Andy left his office and started for the meadow beyond the huge structure. He had been inside it at least a dozen times that day to watch the progress of the work on the Goliath but now, with the crews through for the day, he couldn't resist the urge to step in and gaze in silent admiration at the great hulk that was soon to rule the skies.

The hangar was silent except for a few birds, which made their home there. They wheeled high over the framework of the Goliath, chirping their defiance.

Structural work on the Goliath had been completed several months before and crews of riggers had been busy since then testing and placing the great gas bags which would contain the precious helium, the life-blood of the great craft.

Specifications for the Goliath called for 12 of the large gas bags, which in reality were balloons held captive by the duralumin framework with its covering of sturdy metal cloth. Ten of the large bags had been tested and were in place while the last two would be in place before the end of the week. There would be six in the forward half of the Goliath and six in the after section. In the space between them was the especially designed hold which in peace time would be used for cargo-carrying and in war as the hold in which the Goliath would carry its swarm of fighting planes.

The framework of the Goliath was 850 feet long, sixty-five feet longer than that of the Akron. It's diameter was 135 feet, only three feet more than the Akron but a new manufacturing process had increased the tensile strength of the duralumin used in the Goliath so that it could stand double the strain of the metal used in any previously constructed airship. This process, which had been worked out by Captain Harkins with the assistance of Andy, was one of the great features of the Akron. It was expected that the ship would be able to withstand any storm of less than cyclonic intensity and such an accident as befell the Shenandoah was practically impossible.

The increased strength of the Goliath's framework also allowed the mounting of more powerful engines, which meant greater speed. If the hopes of Andy and the other engineers were realized, the great craft would cruise at 100 miles an hour with a top speed of 120, a decided advantage over any other craft then in service.

Mechanics had been busy the last three weeks mounting the 12 engines which were to provide the power. Each engine was mounted in a separate engine room, completely insulated from the rest of the ship to do away with the danger of fire and lessen noise. Power shafts would project through the side with six propellers on each side.

All of these facts Andy knew by heart and in the silence of the sunset hour he stood in awe before the sky king he was helping to create. In two more months the great doors would roll open, the huge mooring mast, with the Goliath in tow, would waddle out on the concrete runway, and the world's greatest airship would be introduced to its public, some of whom would welcome it enthusiastically while others would gaze at it with questioning eyes, waiting for its trial flights to prove the claims of its builders.

Andy knew that Bert was waiting for him out on the field and he finally forced himself to leave the hangar. He had lived with the Goliath for months and the great ship was almost a part of him.

Mechanics had warmed up Andy's plane and the trim red sportster was ready for the late afternoon spin.

"I thought you weren't going to show up," Bert shouted. "Been in 'talking' with the Goliath?"

Andy grinned and nodded.

"I don't blame you," shouted back Bert. "I go in there every once in a while and just sit down and look at it. Some ship!"

"I'll say," replied Andy. "You'd better get into a sheepskin coat. The air will be a little nippy when we get up five or six thousand feet."

Bert agreed with the suggestion and ran to one of the airplane hangars, which was dwarfed in the lengthening shadows from the Goliath's home. He returned with two coats, one for himself and one for Andy.

The sportster was an Ace two-place biplane with stubby wings, painted silver, and a crimson fuselage. Andy had ordered up dual controls the week before and had promised to give Bert flying instructions whenever they had a spare hour during the spring.

"Let your feet and hands rest lightly on the controls," Andy told his friend, "and whatever you do, don't hang onto them. If you do I may have to clout you over the head with a wrench."

They slipped into their parachute harnesses for Andy was a safe and sane flyer who believed in taking commonsense precautions. Bert climbed into the forward cockpit and Andy slipped into the rear seat.

The motor was warm but he tested it thoroughly before waving to the mechanics to pull the blocks. The sun was a great red disk of flame when they skipped down the meadow and raced into the air.

Bert, who had learned his radio knowledge at a department of commerce station, had never had the opportunity to do much flying until he joined the National Airways radio force and was assigned to Bellevue to take charge of the installation of the equipment on the Goliath. He had arrived the previous fall and during the winter had become Andy's closest friend. They were almost inseparable and Andy, realizing Bert's ambition to become a flyer, had promised to give his friend instructions.

Bert studied each move of the controls and its effect on the maneuvers of the plane. At Andy's suggestion he had read up on the principles of aeronautics and understood the reason for the shifts in the stick and the rudder bar.

At three thousand feet Andy leveled off and waggled the stick, indicating that Bert was to take control. The chunky little radio operator felt his heart go into his throat, but he took a firm grip on the stick and moved it cautiously backward. The nose came up slowly. He moved it ahead. The nose went down ever so slightly. He could fly; he was flying!

He turned around and shouted at Andy in his excitement. The next moment his head was snapped back against his seat. He gasped and jerked around to look at the controls. To his surprise the nose of the plane was in a steep dive and he felt the pit of his stomach start to turn a flip flop.

He knew the thing to do was to pull back on the stick and he did so enthusiastically. The nose came up, the ground disappeared and he found himself staring toward a bank of fleecy clouds that rolled along lazily. His safety belt snapped tight and to his astonishment the ground whirled into view again.

Andy was signaling for the stick and Bert gladly turned over the controls. Andy throttled down and grinned at the radio operator.

"Nice work," he shouted. "I guess you've set a record. At least you're the only fellow I know who looped on his first flight."

"Who what?" cried Bert.

"You looped," replied Andy. "You did a nice piece of flying but I'll bet it was more luck than sense."

"You're right," admitted Bert, who slumped down in his seat, glad enough that Andy was back at the controls.

Andy loafed around the field in easy circles, gradually gaining altitude. The sun was dropping over the horizon and the purple shadows that preceded night were wrapping the countryside in their soft shroud. It was a glorious feeling to be able to take to the air and for the moment forget the pressing cares which he felt around him every minute he was on the ground.

The sportster handled beautifully and Andy found himself at the six thousand foot level almost before he knew it. The air was growing colder and the shadows below deepened rapidly. He throttled down, preparatory to drifting down when he heard a cry from Bert.

The radio operator was shouting and pointing excitedly toward a bank of clouds in the east.

Andy turned and saw a large gray monoplane, traveling fast and high, above the cloud bank. The plane was different from any machine with which he was familiar and he decided to get a closer look at the stranger.

The other machine must have been up 10,000 feet and Andy opened the throttle and sent the Ace scooting upward. At eight thousand he knew the pilot of the other ship had seen him and the gray machine seemed to leap ahead with a sudden burst of speed. They were directly over Bellevue, a prohibited flying area for any except army or National Airways ships, and Andy was curious to know who this flyer was who dared to defy strict air regulations.

The sportster was fast but in less than a minute he knew the other ship was superior in speed. It was a squat, low-winged craft, evidently an all-metal machine and distinctly foreign looking in appearance. Andy made a mental note that he'd get out his design guides when he landed and find out just what make of plane it was that could pull away from his with such apparent ease. It was a useless chase and after five more minutes Andy gave up and swung the Ace back toward Bellevue while the strange ship disappeared in the south.

CHAPTER IV
Danger in the Air

The landing field at Bellevue was shrouded in heavy shadows of the fast-coming night when Andy dropped his Ace sportster down after the futile pursuit of the strange plane.

Merritt Timms, the secret service chief, was waiting for them when the young engineer and the radio operator climbed out of the fuselage.

"Did you get the department of commerce number on the fellow I saw you chasing?" he asked.

"I should say we didn't," replied Andy. "He was too fast for one thing and for another, he didn't have any number on his wings that I could see."

"Outlaw plane?" asked Timms.

"Yes," replied Andy, "and a strange machine. I've never seen one exactly like it. I'm going over to the office and see if I can check up on its design. I've some guide books there that may help us."

"How's the Rubanian agent that was winged earlier this morning?" Bert asked the secret service man.

"He'll come through nicely," replied Timms, "and probably spend about the next five years in a military prison wondering what it is all about."

"Have you had a chance to talk to him?" Andy wanted to know.

"Not yet. I'm going over after supper. Want to come along?"

"Yes," said the young engineer. "How about you, Bert?"

"Count me in," replied the radio operator. "It's too bad he's wounded. I'd like to give him a punch on the nose after all the damage he did to my radio room."

"I don't blame you," chuckled Andy. "He certainly did mess things up but if he had been very intelligent he'd have recognized the installation for the Goliath and have smashed it all to pieces. I guess we've been lucky after all."

When they reached the office Andy dug some reference books on airplane design out of a box and sat down to hunt for a description of the type of craft that he had encountered only a few minutes before.

"I don't think it was an American-made machine," he said, "so we won't waste time hunting there. Let's try the foreign designers first."

British, French, Italian and German divisions failed to furnish any designs similar to the craft he had pictured in his mind's eye.

The Russians had a low-winged monoplane but the wing mounting was too high to answer the description of the craft Andy and Bert had seen.

Andy turned on to the section devoted to the aviation activities and designs of the Rubanian air force. Here was something nearer what he sought. Pictured on one page was a low-winged machine with a streamlined fuselage that very nearly answered the description of the machine he had seen. A footnote added that planes of this type were in production at the Blenkko works near Kratz, the Rubanian capital, but that it was possible minor changes might be made in them when they were put through actual air tests.

"How does this picture strike you?" Andy asked Bert.

"Looks almost exactly like the monoplane we chased," replied the chubby radio operator.

Merritt Timms was intensely interested in the description of the Rubanian plane.

"I'm not surprised," he said, "and I have a hunch we'll find that it was a Rubanian monoplane."

"But how could it get clear over here?" asked Bert.

Timms pointed at the specifications of the monoplane which were printed under the picture.

"Cruising range 7,000 miles," read Bert.

"That would give a good flyer an ample margin to fly from Rubania to Bellevue," said Timms, "and such a feat isn't at all impossible."

"You talk as though you thought the Goliath was in great danger of damage by Rubanian agents," said Bert.

"I don't think now; I know," replied Timms gravely, "for you may be sure that there is danger connected with anything in which Alex Reikoff, dictator of Rubania, is interested. Will you write a brief description of this plane?" he asked, turning to Andy.

"It won't take five minutes," promised Andy.

"Thanks," said Timms. "I'll have a complete description broadcast and we'll be sure to pick him up somewhere. He can't fly on forever and he'll find that disobeying Uncle Sam's orders and flying over a forbidden area is not to be joked with."

Andy wrote a brief but thorough description of the mystery plane and Timms departed to get his message on its way to the broadcasting stations from which a complete description and warning to watch out for the gray monoplane would soon be sent to hundreds of thousands of listeners.

"Think Timms will be able to pick up the flyer of this Rubanian plane?" Bert asked.

"It will be something out of the ordinary if he doesn't," replied Andy. "Timms may be a little slow to get started but once he is on the job he is like a bull dog; he never gives up."

Andy made sure that all of the precious specifications for the Goliath were in the big steel vault before he locked the office. They walked down to the one hotel, where they had made their home while in Bellevue, and cleaned up for supper. A regular mess hall had been built at the plant for the crews, who worked, ate and slept in the buildings erected beside the hangar, but technicians and crew foremen lived at the hotel.

The two long tables in the dining room were well filled when Andy and Bert entered and they were joined a minute or two later by Timms.

"The alarm will be all over the country in another fifteen minutes," said the secret service man, "and we ought to have some news either tonight or the first thing in the morning."

Structural experts, gas experts, motor specialists and expert fitters were at the table and the talk, as it always did, centered on the Goliath, how much progress had been made that day, what they would do the next and to speculation on the exact day the big ship would take the air and what would be its destination on its first official flight.

"Any news on where we'll go on our first long trip?" one of the motor experts asked Andy.

"Sure," replied the young engineer. "We're going to the North pole to exchange mail with the submarine Neptune this summer."

"What!"

"Quit your kidding."

"Say it again."

"You're dreaming."

These and a chorus of similar exclamations greeted Andy's quiet statement. He said it in such a matter-of-fact way that most of the men in the room thought he was joking and he had to repeat his statement two more times before they took him seriously.

"Wait a minute," he added. "I'll read you the telegram that came this afternoon."

He pulled the message from his pocket and read his father's words. When he had finished they were all grave. There was no question now. They were going to the North pole on their first great test of the new airship. Every man in the room knew something of the dangers of a polar flight and they admired Andy's father for his courage in sending the Goliath on such a voyage.

"We'll make a lot of flights to various cities in this country," explained Andy, "before we start on the long trip north so the ship will have a thorough test and we'll know just exactly what she'll do."

"She'll do everything the specifications call for and more too," exclaimed one of the rigging foremen and his words represented the sentiment of every expert in the room for they all had explicit confidence that the Goliath would live up to expectations of her designers and builders.

"When do you think we'll be ready for the test flights?" one of the helium experts asked Andy.

"With the polar trip definitely decided on," replied Andy, "we'll have to be in the air before the end of the next sixty days. That means we can't afford even a single hour's delay on the assembly schedule and we may have to lengthen the shifts in order to get through."

"We'll work 24 hours a day if we have to," said one of the enthusiastic foremen, for after nearly two years of exacting construction work, they were all anxious to see the Goliath test its wings.

The remainder of the supper hour was devoted to heated discussions of the various features of the dirigible, and who would be selected for the crew. Every man in the room hoped that he would get by the final weeding out process and win a permanent berth on the world's largest airship.

Timms was waiting for Andy and Bert after supper in the lobby of the hotel.

"I'm going over and talk to the Rubanian," he said. "Better come along."

They were about to leave the lobby when the program of dance music which was coming in on the radio stopped abruptly for a station announcement.

"Wait a minute," said Bert. "They haven't stopped for the usual station identification. They cut that piece off in the middle."

They went closer to the receiver and it seemed as though the announcer in the station miles away had seen their movement for he started his announcement at once.

"We have just received a special bulletin," said the voice on the ether waves. "A powerful monoplane, of low-winged construction, was sighted just at sunset near Bellevue, Ky. It was flying over a restricted area in violation of department of commerce rules. The machine is fast and slate-gray in color. There appeared to be only one man in the machine and from the description at hand it is evidently of foreign make. It is possible that some European flyer, on a secret long-distance flight, has crossed the Atlantic, and, unaware of the department of commerce regulation, flew over Bellevue, home of the giant airship Goliath. Now, news hounds, get busy and let's see what you can find out about this strange, low-winged monoplane. Any information should be sent direct to this station. Our program of music will continue."

The voice stopped and the dance band which was featured at that hour on the air resumed.

"That ought to get results," said Andy. "Anyone listening in on this program who has heard or seen a plane in the last two hours will undoubtedly send in a report."

"We'll have a lot of misinformation," said Timms, "but a real clue may develop."

"How many stations carried that announcement?" asked Bert.

"The message was sent to about 50 of the major broadcasters," replied Timms, "and every one of them will put it on the air."

"In other words, you covered the whole country," grinned Bert.

"That's what I hoped to do," replied Timms. "Now we'll see just how much value the radio is to the secret service in an emergency when we need the cooperation of the public."

"You'll have something definite before midnight," predicted Bert, who was quick to rise to the defense of his chosen profession.

"It's seven-thirty now," said Andy, glancing at the clock in the lobby. "That gives you four and a half hours."

"That's enough," replied Bert. "If there isn't some real clue by that time I'll buy your suppers tomorrow night."

"And if you win?" Andy asked.

"Then I'll eat supper tomorrow night and the next on you two," grinned Bert.

"I'll buy your suppers for a week," promised Timms, "if we know by midnight where this mysterious plane went."

The doctor in charge of the little emergency hospital which was a part of the National Airways equipment at Bellevue informed them that Dubra, or Cliff Bolton as he had been listed on the payroll, was resting easily and in condition to talk.

The Gerka agent was in a private room and a soldier was seated across the hall, facing the door. The windows were barred and there was little chance that Reikoff's secret agent would go free until Uncle Sam decided he had paid the penalty for his treachery.

Dubra was propped up on pillows, reading an evening paper. He looked up expectantly when they entered but the moment he saw Timms he became sullen. The radio down the hall was plainly audible and Andy recognized the music of the dance band they had heard over the receiving set at the hotel. Unquestionably Dubra had heard the emergency announcement. Andy wondered if there had been any connection between Dubra's attempt to wreck the hangar that morning and the arrival of the Rubanian plane. It was logical to believe that it was part of a carefully laid out plot. He had thought the Goliath safe from an air attack by a jealous foreign country but if the gray plane they had sighted that afternoon proved to be a Rubanian ship, they would have to station several fast army pursuit ships at the field or perhaps install searchlights to ward off any night attack. Possibilities of destruction of the Goliath by an air attack were limitless and Andy grew sick at the thought that the great ship, which represented the labor and love of hundreds of men, was in danger and he looked at the wounded agent of the Gerka with little sympathy.

"How do you feel tonight?" Timms asked Dubra.

"How do you suppose?" was the sullen reply. "I've got two bullet holes in my right leg and another in my left one."

"You're lucky you didn't get one through the heart," replied Timms cheerfully.

"You'll suffer for this outrage," promised Dubra, whose eyes shifted from the secret service agent to Andy, then to Bert, and back to Timms.

"Just as soon as my government learns of this unwarranted attack you'll be in enough trouble to last you the rest of your life."

Dubra's bravado angered Timms, who spoke fiercely.

"Shut up and listen to me," said the secret service agent. "You're a Rubanian resident who posed as a naturalized American. You entered this country unlawfully, you're a secret agent of the Gerka, you attempted to commit murder this morning when you turned on the power of the hangar door and almost killed a half dozen men working on it, you attempted to escape from a military reservation and were shot when you failed to obey repeated commands to halt. A full report of this has been forwarded to the department of justice. You'll be lucky if you don't spend the rest of your life behind the bars at a military prison for remember, Dubra, that military, not civil, courts will deal with your offense and army courts are well known for the severity of their sentences on scoundrels such as you."

The concise, bitter indictment by Timms broke Dubra's spirit of bravado and the agent of the Gerka cringed as he thought of his black future.

"How much were you to be paid for wrecking the hangar?" asked Timms.

Dubra refused to answer.

"How much?" Timms repeated the question.

Still no answer.

"All right, boys," said the secret service agent. "We'll just turn off the light and leave Dubra alone in the dark tonight. He has plenty to think about. Oh, yes, I'll tell the orderly down the hall Dubra's to have no water to drink and any calls from this room are not to be answered."

Timms reached for the light switch and Dubra suddenly changed his mind.

"I'll talk, I'll talk," he cried, "only don't leave me alone in the dark. Something might happen. What do you want to know?"

"Are you the only agent of the Gerka in the plant now?" asked Timms, his words snapping through the quiet of the room.

"Yes," replied Dubra so quickly that the others were convinced he had told the truth.

"And your job was to wreck the hangar and delay construction until another and more powerful agent could get here and finish the job of sabotage against the Goliath?" went on Timms.

This time there was no reply to the question and Dubra turned his face toward the wall.

"I'll give you a minute to make up your mind," said Timms.

The seconds ticked away and there was no sound from any of the four in the small room.

"Make up your mind," warned Timms. "Ten more seconds and the lights go out."

The secret service chief, Andy and Bert turned to leave the room. They were on the threshold when Dubra called them back.

"My job was to wreck the hangar," he confessed, the words coming slowly and evidently with the greatest reluctance.

"Who is going to attempt to wreck the Goliath?" demanded the secret service chief.

"I don't know," whispered Dubra. "The Gerka doesn't work that way. Each of us is assigned a specific task to carry out independent of anyone else."

"Then you don't know who flew that gray monoplane over here this afternoon?" asked Andy.

"I didn't know a monoplane came over."

"Don't lie," said Timms. "If you didn't hear the noise you certainly heard the announcement over the radio just a few minutes ago. Did you expect someone to make a long-distance flight from Rubania for the purpose of destroying the Goliath?"

"I didn't expect anyone," replied Dubra.

"But someone else was to carry out the attack on the Goliath?" persisted Timms.

"Yes," whispered Dubra.

"That's enough for the present," said Timms. "Let's go, boys."

"You promised Dubra some pretty rough treatment if he wouldn't talk," said Bert when they left the hospital.

"It was bluff, pure and simple," smiled Timms, "but he's in a precarious situation and is smart enough to realize that his case will be handled by a court-martial. He's between two fires. If he talks too much his own organization, the Gerka, will revenge themselves on him. If he refuses to talk to us, his penalty will be doubly severe."

"At least the talk with Dubra did one thing," said Andy gravely. "We know for sure that the Goliath is in grave danger and that the man selected to carry out its destruction has not yet arrived at Bellevue."

CHAPTER V
No Clues

On leaving the hospital after questioning the agent of the Gerka, Andy, Bert and the secret service chief walked over to Andy's office. There they discussed plans for additional precautions in the guarding of the Goliath.

"I'm convinced now," said Andy, "that the plane we sighted this afternoon was a Rubanian ship. Either the pilot had made a non-stop flight across the Atlantic or he stopped at some remote place where there was little chance that news of his landing would spread, took on additional fuel, and continued here."

"The fact that we were up sky-larking may have prevented a bomb attack on the Goliath," said Bert.

"That's possible," conceded Timms, "but I doubt that Rubania would dare to use such an open and violent method. An air attack would mean war with popular sentiment of the world with the United States."

"A more likely explanation," said Andy, "is that the agent who is to carry on the actual campaign of destruction against the Goliath arrived in the plane we sighted."

"I'm inclined to believe as you do," Timms told Andy. "Our first step, after doubling the guards around Bellevue, will be to trace this strange craft. I'm hopeful that the radio appeal will bring results."

"I know it will," said Bert confidently.

"Dad will be back within a day or two," said Andy, "and I'll be mighty glad to turn the responsibility of this whole affair over to him. When he's back on the job, we'll take a whirl at finding this unknown agent of the Rubanian Gerka who is to destroy the Goliath," he told Bert.

Timms was busy with a long-distance call to the department of justice in Washington, informing his chief there of the latest development at Bellevue. When he finished, he turned to talk with Andy and Bert.

"Half a dozen army pursuit planes, fully equipped for combat, will drop down here tomorrow morning," he said. "They'll remain until the Goliath is ready to take the air and after that at least two of them will accompany the big ship on all of its trial flights. In addition, an anti-aircraft battery with complete night lighting equipment will arrive before sundown tomorrow."

"That ought to insure us against the success of any attack from the air," said Andy.

"From the air, yes," conceded Timms, "but our danger will lie from an attack within. Everyone who comes on the reservation from now on will be doubly checked."

By ten o'clock that night every possible precaution to safeguard the Goliath had been taken. The military guard around the grounds of the National Airways reservation had been doubled, and extra watchmen had been placed at the hangar. It didn't seem humanly possible for anyone to get within the lines without discovery.

Descriptions of the mysterious plane had been broadcast hourly from the principal radio stations and a mass of information had been received, telegrams having been relayed from the radio stations to which they had been sent.

These messages were checked, one by one, against the large map which had been hung on one wall of Andy's office. On this map had been worked out the probable course of the strange plane. It had come out of the northeast, swung over the home of the Goliath, and then darted away in a southeasterly direction, heading toward the mountains.

Telegrams which failed to indicate a plane in this general line of flight were consigned to the wastebasket. The few that might furnish information were studied carefully but in a majority of cases the description of the plane which the sender of the message had seen failed to come close to that of the machine they sought.

Timms found several messages which appeared worth telephone calls to the senders but on each occasion he was doomed to disappointment.

"I thought you said we'd have some definite news before midnight," he told Bert.

"There's nearly two more hours," replied the radio operator hopefully. "I won't concede defeat until the last minute."

Timms snorted and turned to another handful of telegrams that had just been forwarded. He was half-way through the pile when an exclamation brought Andy and Bert to his side.

"Read that," said the secret service agent, tossing a yellow sheet to them.

The message had been sent from Alden, a small town in the mountains of southeast Kentucky.

"Plane crashed near here early tonight. Description appears to tally with that broadcast. From wreckage it must have been a low-winged monoplane, painted gray. No trace found of pilot." The message was signed by Frank Hacke, editor, the Alden Advocate.

"Who said the radio wouldn't bring results?" demanded Bert. "This message looks like a real tip."

"It does," agreed Timms, reaching for the phone and placing a long distance call for the editor of the Alden paper.

Half an hour elapsed before the operator was able to get the call through and Timms fumed with impatience. When the wire was finally cleared for his conversation, he fairly leaped at the telephone. Question after question was fired over the wire and Andy and Bert, from the very tenseness of Timms' attitude, knew that the secret service man was getting valuable information. His final words were highly significant.

"I'll be there as soon as possible. If I can fly in, have auto lights turned on to mark the boundaries of a field that is safe for a landing."

Timms banged the receiver on the hook and turned to Andy and Bert.

"We've found the wreckage of the gray plane," he said. "It smacked into the side of a mountain about three miles from Alden. The editor of the paper was one of the first ones to reach the scene but they were unable to find any trace of the pilot. We've got to get to Alden at once for we mustn't let that flyer get away. He's the man who is slated to bring about the actual destruction of the Goliath."

The words rang through Andy's head. The pilot had somehow escaped in the crash. It was possible to crack up a ship without injury but it was more likely that the man they sought had jumped while the plane was in flight, drifting down in his chute and leaving the plane to crash to its own destruction.

Andy heard Timms asking if he could fly him to Alden that night. He replied almost mechanically and then hastened out of the office and down the field to rout out several mechanics, who rolled his red sportster out on the concrete apron and checked it thoroughly. The motor sent echoes blasting through the stillness of the night as Andy himself tested it.

He was joined several minutes later by Bert and the secret service agent.

Timms climbed into the forward cockpit and Bert started to crowd in with him.

"Sorry, Bert," called Andy. "You'll have to stay on the ground this trip. The Ace is only a two-place job and I can't afford to overtax its capacity tonight. I'll need all my speed and climbing ability in dodging over the mountains."

Bert was keenly disappointed but he knew the truth of Andy's words and he dropped back to the ground.

"I'll warn Alden that you're coming by air," he said, "and they'll be sure to have a field marked in some way."

"Fine," yelled Andy. "See you tomorrow."

Flame licked around the exhaust vent of the motor as Andy opened the throttle. The Ace came to life with a quick flirt of its tail. The riding lights gleamed sharply in the night; then were swallowed in the haze of dirt swept up from the field by the wash of the propeller.

Alden was just a little under an hour of fast flying from Bellevue and Andy opened the Ace up until they were skimming through the half clear night at a hundred and twenty miles an hour. The lights of Bellevue disappeared as if blotted out by the hand of an unseen giant and they were alone in the sky.

Andy had plotted a compass course and he followed it closely for Alden was tucked away in the mountains and he could easily miss the village if slightly off course.

By the end of the first half hour the clouds had cleared and a thin moon tried vainly to dissipate the blackness of the night. Lights on the ground were few and far between with midnight almost at hand. The air was raw and Andy snuggled deeper into the sheepskin he had donned for the trip. He checked the time and compass again. Alden should show on the horizon any moment if his calculations were correct. Another two minutes passed and he sighted a glow of light to the left. He nosed the Ace over and dropped lower.

Lights below flashed on and off. He blinked his riding lights and those on the ground answered. There was no way of detecting the direction of the light wind and Andy had to take a chance that there were no bad ground currents. He skimmed over the field to determine its length. It appeared to be on a side-hill for level stretches of land were few and far between in that section of the state. The field was long enough for an easy landing and he cut the motor and slid down the invisible trail.

He was going in too fast and he opened the throttle and zoomed into the sky for another try. The second time he stalled all the way down, drifted over the top of the car whose lights marked the near end of the field, and dropped to an easy landing. He swung the Ace around and taxied back over the uneven field. A group was waiting when they climbed down from the cockpits.

Fred Hacke, the editor, stepped up and introduced himself. With him was Sheriff Jud Barnes, a six foot two man of the mountains who was proud of his great, booming voice.

"Get in my car," said the sheriff, "and I'll run you over to the hill where that airplane busted."

For half an hour they bounced over a rough mountain road and were glad enough when the sheriff stopped the car and led the way through a patch of timber. The grade was steep and they were compelled to rest several times. Finally they came to a small clearing, crossed this and just beyond saw a darker mass against the trees. The sheriff turned his flashlight on a tangled pile of cloth and metal, the broken remnants of the machine Andy had chased only a few hours before.

The editor and his party came up and they made a thorough inspection of the wreckage. Motor numbers and the name of the maker had been filed away, the plates on the fuselage had been removed and every means of absolute identification taken off. In spite of this Andy and the secret service agent were positive that the plane was of Rubanian make and that an agent of the Gerka had been at the controls when it had been sighted at Bellevue.

"We haven't found the flyer yet," said the sheriff. "Maybe he spilled out somewhere before the wreck. We'll search the hills in the morning."

"I don't think it will do any good," replied Andy. "The chap that was flying this machine undoubtedly took to his parachute. He may have landed some miles away. If the controls were locked before he jumped, the ship could have cruised alone for three or four minutes on a quiet night like this."

"We'll have a look anyway," said the sheriff, and Andy and Timms decided to remain at least until noon to see if the searching parties discovered anything of importance.

They returned to Alden, took a room at the hotel, and slept until dawn. Andy went out to the field where they had landed and went over the Ace carefully while Timms accompanied the sheriff into the hills.

The secret service agent returned at noon and announced that the search had proved fruitless. There were no more clues, either at the scene of the wreck or in the nearby hills, and they decided to return to Bellevue at once.

Andy got the Ace off the improvised airport without trouble and they headed for home through the bright rays of the spring sun. As they sped over the tree-covered hills, Andy flew mechanically, his mind busy on the new problem which confronted them. There was no question now. The Goliath was in serious danger and every means at their command must be used to protect the great airship, destruction of which would mean the ruin of the National Airways, which had invested millions in its construction. But more than the mere financial loss which it would mean was the month of labor by the loyal crew, the years of planning on the part of his father and Captain Harkins, and his own love for the great craft.

An attack from the air was improbable for the Rubanian agent had wrecked his own plane deliberately. Whatever happened would be caused by someone who had easy access to the hangar and Andy resolved that he would be doubly vigilant in the days to come.

CHAPTER VI
The Night Alarm

When Andy taxied the Ace across the field at Bellevue and up to the concrete apron, he found Bert waiting for him. The radio operator was nearly bursting with curiosity to learn what Andy and the secret service chief had found at Alden.

"Control yourself, Bert, control yourself," grinned Andy as he hoisted himself out of the cockpit and slid to the ground.

"You can't blame me for being curious," replied Bert, "when I've been marooned here for the last twelve hours while you've been chasing excitement all over southeastern Kentucky."

"That's just it," said Andy. "We were only chasing. We didn't find a thing to give us thrill."

"No trace of the mysterious flyer?" asked Bert.

"Nary a sign," replied Andy. "We found where his plane had attempted to bore its way through the side of a hill but he had evidently dropped out some time before in his chute. He's probably securely hidden waiting for a chance to bring about the destruction of the Goliath."

"That won't be an easy thing to accomplish," said Bert. "The guard lines have been tightened so a bird can hardly fly over them without being stopped. The army planes came in before noon and any flyer who violates the department of commerce regulations by flying over this air reservation will find a handful of slugs singing through his wings."

Andy nodded grimly as he looked at the group of army machines in front of a hangar further down the field.

"We're ready for business now," he said. "I'd like to meet the officer in command."

"He's a fine fellow," enthused Bert. "Not much older than we are. His name is Lieutenant Jim Crummit of Selfridge Field, Mich. He's one of the ace pursuit flyers of the air force and the rest of the fellows with him are not far behind when it comes to handling a plane with a machine gun on the business end of it. They're just itching for something to happen."

"I'm afraid they'll be disappointed," said Merritt Timms, who had just emerged from the cockpit, having experienced some trouble in unfastening his safety belt. "They would have had plenty of fun if they had been here yesterday but from now on the game will be played on the ground or aboard the Goliath when it goes on its trial flights."

"Here comes Lieutenant Crummit now," said Bert, stepping forward to greet the tall young officer in command of the detachment from Selfridge Field.

Bert introduced the lieutenant to Andy and the secret service agent, who cordially welcomed the army man to Bellevue.

"Our field is a little bumpy but we'll try and make up in hospitality what we lack in air accommodations," said Andy.

"The field is O.K.," smiled Lieutenant Crummit. "A couple of the boys came in too fast and bounced a little high but they'll soon get over that. We're all glad to be here where we can watch the completion of the Goliath."

"I understand several ships will be detailed to accompany us on all trial flights," said Andy.

"Those are the orders direct from Washington," said the lieutenant. "Now, somebody tell me what all the fuss is about?"

They walked over to the office where Andy and the secret service chief explained in detail every event of the preceding twenty-four hours.

"That does look serious," said Lieutenant Crummit, "especially since you have an admission from the agent of the Gerka you caught here that an attempt was to be made to destroy the Goliath. At least you can feel reasonably safe from an air attack. Anti-aircraft equipment with night lights will be in tonight and the unit also carries special microphones for the detection of planes in flight. Any craft approaching here will be known while it is miles away and we can give it a warm reception."

Assignment of the army flyers to quarters had been held up pending Andy's return and he arranged for them to have accommodations at the hotel, six of the construction foremen agreeing to give up their double rooms and move over to the company houses on the reservation proper.

It was late afternoon before Andy was alone in his office with an opportunity to go over the day's mail There were several important looking letters on top but he shuffled through the stack until he came to one in his father's familiar writing. He slit it open and read it eagerly. It was with a real feeling of relief that he learned his father and Captain Harkins would return late the next day, coming in on a special National Airways plane. His father wrote that final arrangements had been finished for all of the delicate apparatus which was to go into the control room of the Goliath and that, unless there were unforeseen developments, everything was now lined up so that construction would be completed ahead of schedule.

The afternoon freight train brought the anti-aircraft unit, with its searchlights, field pieces and other equipment. The twenty-five men of this company were housed in company quarters, which had been vacated only the week before by a crew which had finished its work.

Before nightfall Bellevue had been turned into a truly military camp with its strict guard around the grounds of the National Airways plant, the army planes ready to take the air at any time of day or night, and the great searchlights, crouching under their shrouds of canvas, eager to send their searing blue-white beams tracing through the night sky.

"When a fellow looks over the field now," said Bert as they walked to the hotel for supper, "he realizes just how valuable the Goliath is to Uncle Sam."

"We've got the jump on them now," said Andy. "Dubra failed in his attempt to damage the hangar and is now in our hands. That means the 'inside man' on whom Reikoff had counted for cooperation with this newcomer from Rubania is out of the picture and our guard lines have been tightened until it is almost physically impossible for anyone to get through. But even with all those precautions, we'll continue to keep our eyes and ears open."

Supper that night was a jolly affair, with introductions of Lieutenant Crummit and his companions to the engineers and foremen in charge of the building of the Goliath. The army flyers were keenly interested in the construction of the great dirigible and Andy enjoyed Lieutenant Crummit's practical inquiries on the stability of the big gas bag, what it was expected to do when in the air and its availability for war-time use.

"We know in a general way," he said, "but nothing very definite has appeared on the actual capability of the craft."

Andy had an enthusiastic second in Bert and they went over a complete outline of the Goliath and its range, both in peace and war times, for the army men. By the time they were through, supper was over and the group broke up in twos and threes and straggled into the lobby of the old-fashioned hotel. The air was chilly and a great fire had been built in the fireplace. Lights were low and there was a general spirit of comradeship in the room. The radio had ceased its accustomed blare and a really excellent orchestra, devoid of the usual advertising propaganda, was playing familiar airs.

Someone started humming and in another minute the room was filled with lusty voices that took up the refrain. For half an hour they enjoyed the impromptu concert until a messenger boy came in with a telegram for Bert.

The young radio operator looked surprised as he fingered the yellow envelope, turning it over as though half expecting to find the address of the sender on the back.

"Now who under the sun could be telegraphing me?" he asked.

"Better open it and find out," suggested Andy.

"A most original proposal," replied Bert tartly. "It's from Harry Curtis," he cried as he read the message. "He's going to the North pole as radio operator for Gilbert Mathews on the submarine Neptune."

"My gosh," Bert continued in the same breath. "That means we'll meet Harry at the North pole sometime this summer."

"Well, that is a coincidence," said Andy, who had met Harry Curtis the year before. Bert and Harry had served the department of commerce together and were close friends, a friendship which had not dimmed by their separation. Andy had taken a liking to Harry on their first meeting. Harry had visited at Bellevue during the preceding summer and their friendship had developed rapidly.

"What a thrill we'll have saying 'hello' to each other in the Arctic," he said.

"But that isn't all," added Bert. "It seems that your father and Mathews have agreed to keep in touch with each other by radio so Harry has been ordered here to check up on our radio equipment with me. We'll arrange for complete synchronization of the sets so that we'll be able to get through to each other at any time."

"That sounds like Dad," said Andy. "He's always looking ahead and planning for any emergency. It will take careful timing to bring both the Neptune and the Goliath to the pole at the same time. Believe me, Bert, you're going to have an important job when the Goliath finally sticks her nose into the air and heads north."

"I'm commencing to realize how really important it is," said Bert soberly.

"Hey, wait a minute," he added. "I almost forgot one of the most important parts of this telegram. Harry said he was starting at once for Bellevue."

"Good," said Andy. "Where was the message sent from?"

"New York," replied Bert.

"That means it will be tomorrow afternoon before he arrives," reasoned Andy as he mentally outlined the train schedules between the metropolis and the isolated Kentucky valley.

The group in the hotel lobby broke up, most of the men going to their rooms to write letters or read while a few gathered around a chess board. Andy had some correspondence to finish and he walked down to his office. Reports for the day showed better than average progress had been made on the Goliath and he wrote these into the permanent record of the construction of the mammoth craft.

For an hour he worked at his desk, catching up on the mail which had come in that morning. All of it was routine with the exception of another short notice from the war department that Herman Blatz, the civilian observer from Friedrichshafen, would arrive at Bellevue the next day. It added that every courtesy of the National Airways plant should be made available to the newcomer.

The note irritated Andy. He was inclined to be suspicious of any newcomer now but he realized that he would have to master that feeling for they were deeply indebted to Doctor Eckener for his many contributions to the advancement of dirigibles. Andy filed the letter from the war department and was about to leave his office and return to the hotel when the blast of a siren cracked the night wide open. It was shrill, penetrating, alarming—the kind of noise that creeps up and down the spine and makes the short hair at the back of the neck stand straight up.

Lights flashed on in the anti-aircraft battery down the field. Hangar doors swung open. Mechanics popped out of beds and into their clothes. Canvas hoods were ripped off the searchlights and the dynamos hummed with energy.

The microphones had picked up the sound of an approaching airplane. Propellers of the army planes spun. Flame whimpered around the exhaust stacks. Ammunition belts were fed into the black, deadly little guns.

Andy ran along the line of fighting planes. They were poised; eager for the word to go. Every other light in Bellevue had been put out. There was only the occasional flicker of the exhaust of one of the waiting planes. He felt out of the picture; the army was in command. He stopped beside Lieutenant Crummit's plane and the army officer leaned down.

"Room enough in here if you want to pile in and see this shindig," he shouted.

The invitation was followed by the acceptance in action and Andy vaulted into the cockpit of the speedy fighter. It was lucky they were both slender but even then it was a tight squeeze.

"How do you know when to go?" asked Andy.

"The plane was ten miles away and heading this way when the 'mike' picked it up," replied Lieut. Crummit. He glanced at his wrist watch.

"The searchlights will go on in ten more seconds. We'll start up the minute they fasten on anything."

The words were hardly out of his mouth when the night awoke to a blue-white brilliance as the searchlights sent their beams soaring into the sky. Back and forth moved the giant fingers of light, each one covering a certain area. Any plane near the reservation was certain of detection.

There was a cry from Lieutenant Crummit.

"There it is," he shouted as he gunned the pursuit ship. It seemed to Andy that they jumped straight into the air, so fast was the rise of their craft. Up and up they went, the brilliant light from below pointing an unerring path toward the plane they sought. It was a black biplane, fast and streamlined.

The pilot was twisting and turning to get away from the pursuing beams of light but his task was useless with the army pursuit ships rising from below in an angry swarm.

They were at two thousand feet in no time and level with the craft they sought. Lieutenant Crummit pressed the trigger of his machine gun and a stream of tracer bullets coursed through the night, singing past the machine ahead.

Andy saw the pilot turn a desperate, terror-stricken face in their direction. Someone in the forward cockpit was waving. They drew closer. The plane was giving up. A white handkerchief was being waved by the passenger.

Lieutenant Crummit drew closer and signaled for the black biplane to follow him down. The pilot waggled his wings to indicate that he understood the order and they began the strange descent, Lieutenant Crummit and Andy in the leading plane, then the strange biplane followed by the five other army ships.

The operators of the searchlights changed the direction of their beams, turning them on the field to make it easy for the night landing.

As soon as their own plane had stopped rolling, Andy leaped out and ran toward the black biplane. Lieutenant Crummit was only one stride behind and in his right hand he carried a service automatic.

Andy was astounded to hear a familiar voice from the black plane.

"What kind of a reception is this?" was the demand and he looked up into the face of Harry Curtis, radio operator of the Neptune, whom they had not expected until the following day at the earliest.

"Who is this fellow?" Lieutenant Crummit wanted to know.

Andy explained that Harry had been ordered to Bellevue to plan for the radio communication between the Goliath and Neptune during their Arctic trips and Lieutenant Crummit broke into a broad smile.

"At least we gave you a real army welcome," he chuckled. "It's lucky one of the other boys didn't reach you first, though. This is restricted flying territory and he might not have sent his first burst of tracers alongside just as a warning."

"I was scared to death," confessed Harry, who had climbed down from the plane just in time to receive a hearty greeting from Bert. "Believe me I sure scrambled around trying to get a handkerchief out of my pants pocket."

The civilian pilot of Harry's plane came in for a severe reprimand from Lieutenant Crummit, who warned him not to repeat the offense again.

Dynamos for the searchlights were turned off, planes wheeled back into the hangars and Bellevue turned on its lights once more. They had had their first night alarm and the army men on the job had proved their ability to handle the emergency.

CHAPTER VII
Suspicions

Andy, Bert and Harry talked until far into the night, discussing the proposed meeting of the Goliath and the submarine Neptune at the North Pole.

"There's no doubt in my mind," said Andy, "that the Goliath will be able to make the trip on schedule. What I'm wondering about is the tin fish."

"You can cease worrying right now," replied Harry. "The Neptune isn't a cast-off navy submarine refitted for a polar cruise. It's a long-distance underwater cruiser of the latest type and only a multi-millionaire explorer like Gilbert Mathews could afford to operate such a craft. Believe me, it's some boat."

"And believe me," added Bert, "the Goliath is some airship. Wait until you see it in the daylight. Its size will fairly take your breath away."

"I can believe you easily enough," replied Harry, "for the eastern newspapers have been carrying a great many feature stories about the Goliath. Only the National Airways haven't been giving out a lot of actual facts and with reporters barred from the plant here, they've had to guess at part of the stories they've been printing. Everyone is anxious for an actual view of the big ship."

"You'll be in on all of the previews," Andy promised, "and if you stay with us long enough I can promise you several trial flights."

"Bert and I will probably be through in a month," said Harry. "Then I'll have to hop down to Brooklyn and make the final adjustments on the set aboard the Neptune. After that's done I may be able to get back here for a few days. I'd certainly like to go along on the trial runs."

There were no more alarms that night and finally the three young enthusiasts ceased talking and dropped into deep slumber.

The next day was clear with a warm sun and a definite note of spring was in the air. Birds, on their northward flight, wheeled over the hangar and the grass was a fresher, brighter green.

Andy made the rounds at the hangar with Harry, an eager observer, at his side. Assembly of the main gondola was starting, a task which Andy was to personally supervise. In this large car would be located the control room and the passengers quarters with their individual staterooms, dining salons and lounging quarters. Quarters for the crew were built inside the hull and in the middle of the ship between the banks of gas cells.

Harry was properly impressed with the size of the Goliath and exclaimed at the engineering progress which had been made in its construction.

Andy explained how the double-strength duralumin had increased the strength of the frame to such a point that a disaster such as had befallen the Shenandoah could not strike the Goliath.

"How many passengers will you be able to carry when the ship goes into transcontinental service?" Harry asked.

"We'll have sleeping accommodations for 200," replied Andy, "and during daytime runs between large cities will be able to carry an extra 100."

"Will the fares be pretty stiff?" asked Harry. "Not as much as you would expect. They will average railroad plus Pullman."

"In that case," said Harry, "you can be sure of capacity business for a good many years."

"We'll have to if National Airways is to break even on the operation of the Goliath," said Andy.

Bert, who had remained in the office to check over blueprints on an especially complicated piece of radio equipment for the Goliath, hurried up.

"Andy," he said. "Herman Blatz is here."

"Who?" asked Andy.

"Blatz," repeated Bert, "Herman Blatz. He's the civilian observer from Friedrichshafen."

"Of course," grinned Andy. "I'd forgotten the name for a moment. What does he look like?"

"Fine looking sort of a fellow," replied Bert. "He's just about our own age; not quite as tall as you are and dark; brown eyes and hair that is almost coal black."

"If you don't mind running back to the office," said Andy, "tell him that I'll be along presently. I want to make sure that the assembly of the gondola starts smoothly."

Andy became engrossed in the direction of the subforemen and their crews and he even forgot Harry, much less the newcomer who was waiting for him in the office.

An hour later Bert returned.

"What's the idea?" he demanded. "I thought you said you'd be along right away. Blatz has been cooling his heels for more than an hour."

"Sorry," grinned Andy, who had been helping with the assembly. "I was so interested I forgot all about him. I'll come along with you."

The young engineer crawled out from beneath the duralumin frame on which he had been working, wiped his hands on a piece of waste, brushed off his dungarees, the universal uniform of engineers, foremen and mechanics at the Bellevue plant.

Andy stepped into his office, blinked his eyes to accustom them to the dark interior, and looked into the face of Lieut. Serge Larko, secret agent of Alexis Reikoff's Grega, who had been assigned the task of bringing about the destruction of the Goliath. But Andy was to know the visitor as Herman Blatz, civilian observer from Friedrichshafen, and he stepped forward with a cordial greeting.

"We shall be delighted to have you with us," said Andy, "and I must apologize for my tardiness in greeting you. We have just started the assembly of the main gondola and I have been giving it my personal supervision."

"The Goliath is that near completion?" asked Lieutenant Larko, who from here on we shall speak of in his new role as Herman Blatz.

"We'll be making trial flights in less than two months," replied Andy enthusiastically.

"It was well that I arrived at this time," said Blatz, "for I will be able to remain long enough for the trial flights."

"The war department communications indicated that you would probably accompany us on the test trips," said Andy.

"Yes," replied Blatz. "Europe is greatly interested in the Goliath and I feel it a rare privilege that I have been assigned here."

The young German's pronunciation of English was clear and precise, his words close-clipped in the Teuton manner.

"I understand that you have been at Friedrichshafen some time," said Andy.

"Yes," replied Blatz, who dreaded questions about the Germany airship base. He wondered how much this young American might really know about him; how much he might suspect for he had sensed instantly that Andy was suspicious of every newcomer.

"I spent a year at Friedrichshafen," said Andy. "It is possible that we know a number of the same men there. Do you recall Bauer and Schillig, who were the aces of the navigation class in 1929?"

"The names are familiar," replied Blatz, "but I went through navigation the preceding year." Harry and Bert came into the office and Andy introduced the German expert and the radio operator of the Neptune.

"You are going to carry a submarine radio operator on an airship?" asked Blatz.

"Oh, no," replied Bert quickly. He was about to explain that the Goliath and the Neptune were to meet at the North pole that summer but a warning glance from Andy silenced him, and he added, rather lamely.

"Harry and I were department of commerce operators and he's down here helping me with the final assembly of the set for the Goliath."

"Very fortunate. I'm sure," said Blatz.

"You understand," said Andy, "that there are certain construction secrets which I can not divulge?"

"Of course," replied Blatz, "and I assure you that you need have no worry on that score."

Andy suggested that they make a tour of the plant and Blatz readily assented for he was anxious to see the Goliath. He had received some idea of the size when he had flown over at sunset two days before and glimpsed the hangar. As they walked toward the huge structure, he wondered who had chased him in the red plane. He had been tired after the long flight across the Atlantic and had lost his way after striking the Atlantic coast. He had not intended coming as close to Bellevue but when he finally got his bearings he was less than a hundred miles away and he could not resist the temptation. But it had been a foolish move for a little red plane had darted out of the shadows below and pushed him hard before he had escaped into the coming night. Another hundred miles and he had slipped out of the cockpit of the Blenkko which had served him so faithfully in the long flight from Rubania, and had dropped through the night in his chute. He had clutched a suitcase with fresh clothes and his precious identification papers as Herman Blatz in his arms.

The landing had been easy and after washing the grime of the long flight off in a nearby creek, he had changed clothes; then burned his old clothes, the parachute and the suitcase. Into the fire had gone everything which would identify him as Lieut. Serge Larko of the Rubanian air force on special duty as an agent of the Gerka. Out of the timber and onto the highway had stepped Herman Blatz, who had hitch-hiked to the nearest town where he had rested for a day, bought a fresh wardrobe, and then continued by train and auto to Bellevue.

A suppressed excitement gripped his whole being He had done the seemingly impossible, flown the Atlantic and made his way into this carefully guarded dirigible plant, thanks to the clever subterfuge Reikoff must have used in getting permission for a civilian observer to visit

Bellevue. He would get in touch with Boris Dubra, the mechanic who was a member of the Gerka, at the first opportunity.

They entered the hangar and Blatz stopped involuntarily. Andy had expected that reaction and it told him that the newcomer was a true airman for the majestic bulk of the Goliath usually struck those who were viewing it for the first time speechless.

"It's inspiring," gasped Blatz. "I never dreamed an airship could be so large."

"Of course it looks larger in the hangar than it really is," said Andy, "but we're rather proud of the Goliath."

"Friedrichshafen has never done anything like it," said Andy. "Or, for that matter, has anyone else in the world."

"You're right," nodded Blatz. "I wonder that you ever tore yourself away from here and came out to meet me."

"I've just about lived with the Goliath," admitted Andy, "for Dad and Captain Harkins have been forced to make many trips to see about materials. They will return this afternoon to greet you."

"I look forward to meeting two such famous men. The honor is great."

They continued through the hangar, Andy pointing out and explaining the progress which had been made on the component parts of the great airship.

"One of the pleasantest years of my life," said Andy, "was the one passed at Friedrichshafen. I recall the day I went up in one of the small dirigibles, the Strassburg, I believe. Karl Staab was at the controls and a wind squall hit us. It pushed us clear across Lake Constance and we were lucky to get home the same day. Karl was a great joker but a wonderful navigator despite that."

"Yes, you're quite right," nodded Blatz. "He always enjoyed a good laugh."

Andy's eyes narrowed and he looked closely at the newcomer. He started to say something; then thought better of it and quickly switched the conversation from reminiscences of days at Friedrichshafen to the present.

Andy, Bert, Harry and Blatz lunched together at the hotel where Andy introduced the German expert to the heads of the construction staff at Bellevue. Blatz was accorded a warm welcome and after lunch resumed his tour of the plant with Andy.

In mid-afternoon a National Airways plane dropped in from the north. The army flyers, warned of its coming, did not roar into the sky in angry pursuit, but squatted beside their planes and watched the cabin monoplane skid to a stop in front of one of the smaller hangars.

Andy excused himself and ran toward the plane. The first man out of the cabin was his father, and Andy received an affectionate greeting.

"Everything going O.K. son?" asked the vice president of the National Airways.

"We've had a little excitement. Dad," replied Andy, "but it didn't affect the work on the Goliath. We're well ahead of schedule."

"Fine," replied Andy's father. "We'll need all of the extra time for trial flights before we start our northward trip."

"Then it's definitely settled that we'll meet the Neptune at the North pole?"

"Very definitely settled," replied Charles. High. "The contracts were signed yesterday. Captain Harkins has our copies with him."

The tall, bronzed airman who was the chief designer and captain of the Goliath stepped out of the cabin of the monoplane.

"Hello, Andy," he said, extending his hand for a cordial greeting. "Have you started the assembly of the main gondola?"

"Work got under way on that project this morning," replied Andy, "and the crews are making unusually good time."

"I've decided on several minor changes," said Captain Harkins, "but they need not delay the general construction work on the main car."

As they walked toward the office buildings, Andy briefly explained what had happened during their absence, how Dubra had attempted to damage the hangar, the passage and pursuit of the foreign plane, the arrival of the army patrols and Dubra's admission that an attempt was under way to destroy the Goliath.

"The wonder of it is," said Andy's father, "that some foreign power hasn't made the attempt before. Now that we are fore-warned, there is little chance of success in damaging the big ship."

Andy saw Herman Blatz waiting for him some distance away and he spoke to his father and Captain Harkins in low tones, explaining that Blatz had been sent to Bellevue on special orders of the war department.

"I can see no objection to that," said Captain Harkins. "Doctor Eckener at Friedrichshafen has placed us deeply in his debt through suggestions on the improvement of our general design and one of his observers is welcome as far as I am concerned."

"National Airways feels the same way," added Andy's father.

Andy took his father and Captain Harkins over to Blatz where he made the necessary introductions. They were soon engaged in a spirited discussion of the improvements in aircraft building which were represented in the Goliath and Andy left them to walk back to his own office.

The arrival of Blatz had disturbed him strangely. He had hoped that he would be able to welcome the newcomer with real cordiality but instead he found a mounting barrier of resentment rising between himself and the German.

Blatz' story didn't ring true. Andy had tested him that afternoon when he had recalled the incident at Friedrichshafen when he and Karl Staab had been blown across Lake Constance in the old Strassburg. Blatz had recalled knowing Staab when, in reality, there was no such navigator at Friedrichshafen. The whole story and the name had been invented by Andy to test Blatz. If, as he claimed, he had been connected with the Friedrichshafen plant for a number of years, he could not have remembered a man who did not exist. Blatz had agreed too readily. Andy's suspicions were aroused and he promised himself an investigation.

CHAPTER VIII
Mysterious Moves

When Herman Blatz, alias Lieut. Serge Larko of the Rubanian secret police, was alone in his room late that afternoon preparing for supper, he was torn between conflicting emotions. He had reached Bellevue safely. He was even inside the plant of the National Airways, accepted as a German civilian observer. The opportunity for him to wreck the Goliath might present itself at any moment but two mighty emotional forces were at work. One was his inherent love for anything man-made that could conquer the elements. Only that afternoon he had viewed the greatest of all airships and he quailed inwardly at the thought that his task was to destroy the mighty craft.

He heard the call for supper and descended to the dining room where he was seated at the head table with Andy, Bert, Harry, Andy's father and Captain Harkins. There was a vacant chair at his left and he wondered who the late-comer would be.

Conversation at the table was devoted almost solely to topics centering around the Goliath and the young Rubanian airman reveled in the sheer joy it brought him. For the time he forgot his ominous mission and was light-hearted and gay.

Supper was half over when a quiet man slipped into the chair beside him. Andy turned and introduced the late arrival.

"Mr. Blatz," he said, "I want you to know Merritt Timms, chief of the secret service agents here."

Blatz acknowledged the introduction mechanically and Andy, watching his every move and facial expression, failed to see any note of alarm. It was well for Blatz that Andy's eyes could not penetrate beneath the surface for Blatz's mind was working rapidly.

The chief of the secret service agents at Bellevue seated beside him! Had he aroused suspicion already? Had there been a slip somewhere along the line; could these alert Americans know his identity and be playing with him, waiting for him to make a slip so they could send him to some military prison?

He knew the careful workings of the Gerka and he doubted that a slip had been made. That thought gave him some reassurance and his gay attitude returned.

They finished the meal and chairs were pushed back.

"I'm going over to the hospital," said Timms to Andy. "Want to go along and hear what Dubra has to say?"

Andy darted a glance at Blatz. He saw the civilian observer start ever so slightly. It was hardly more than a tremor but it helped to verify Andy's suspicions.

"I'll go," he replied. "Perhaps Blatz here would like to come with us?"

"Yes, of course," replied the other. "Some mechanic hurt?"

"A little," replied Timms. "A couple of bullets hurt him. He was an agent of the Gerka, Rubanian secret police organization, planted here to damage the hangar. He failed and the guards didn't miss when he tried to escape."

"I'm surprised to hear that," said Blatz. "I didn't suppose anyone would direct any destructive efforts toward the Goliath."

"We'll be surprised if anyone else does," said Timms, "for we know that Alex Reikoff, dictator of Rubania, would like nothing better than to hear about the destruction of the Goliath. As a result, we've taken every precaution that is humanly possible."

"That is wise," said Blatz, "for in Europe we have come to fear Reikoff as a menace to the peace of the world."

They were in the doorway of the hospital now and Blatz saw Andy's keen blue eyes boring into him, probing as though questioning the truth of his words. He felt that his answers, especially the reference to Reikoff as a menace, had been well put.

A slight infection had set in on Dubra's right leg and the Rubanian was restless with pain.

"Hello, Dubra," said the secret service chief. "Just dropped in to see how you are getting along."

"They're killing me," cried the man on the bed. "My leg hurts so."

"They're doing no such thing," replied Timms. "The doctor here is making every effort to save your worthless life. Have you got anything else to add to what you said the other night?"

Dubra's eyes were bright with fever but his mind was clear and he shook his head.

Blatz kept well in the background. He had lost the ally Reikoff had told him he would have. Dubra, over-anxious to cause harm, had been caught and wounded. His usefulness as an agent of destruction was at an end and Blatz would have to go on alone. Perhaps it would be easier that way.

There was no more information to be had from the wounded Rubanian and they left the hospital. When they returned to the hotel, Blatz excused himself and went to his room. Timms signified his intention to do likewise but changed his mind when Andy insisted that they take a walk together.

"What's the idea?" the secret service chief asked when they were well away from the hotel and walking in the open.

"It's Blatz," said Andy. "There's something about him that doesn't ring true."

The assistant pilot of the Goliath related the incident of the afternoon with the fake story of the adventure at Friedrichshafen.

"That sounds a little fishy," admitted Timms, "but that's not enough to accuse a man of being a spy."

"I realize that," admitted Andy, "but you should have seen him tonight when you asked me if I wanted to go to the hospital and see Dubra. Blatz's face paled and he trembled ever so slightly. No one else noticed it but I had been watching him closely."

"Still there is nothing definite," insisted Timms.

"There's enough so that I'm not going to let him get very far away from me," replied Andy. "Can't you start a quiet tracer through the secret service; find out where and when he landed; how he came to receive the permission from the war department and anything else your people in Europe can dig up?"

"It might be rather serious if your suspicions proved unfounded," said Timms.

"I'm willing to take the risk," replied Andy.

"Then I'll see what can be done," promised the secret service chief.

Events during the next month at Bellevue were quiet enough. Andy kept a close watch of Blatz, but the German observer's conduct was model. He confined his activities solely to observance and taking notes on the parts of the Goliath to which he was allowed access and he made no move to delve into the military secrets which were a part of the giant craft.

Bert and Harry had been busy with the installation of the intricate radio equipment which was a part of the Goliath. Late in April they completed their joint task and Bert announced that the communications apparatus was ready.

Assembly of the gondola had been completed, motor crews were busy tuning up the 12 giant engines which were to provide the power and fitters worked overtime on the installation of the luxurious furnishings of the lounge and sleeping quarters in the passenger cabins.

The gondola of the Goliath was a two-deck affair. In the fore part of the lower deck was the control and operations room with the communications room just behind. The main lounge was located on this deck with the dining room and the chef's quarters at the rear of the gondola. An enclosed promenade deck, encircled the lounge and dining room. The upper deck was devoted solely to passenger cabins, which were fitted like the staterooms of a Pullman. Every modern convenience for the comfort of travelers had been built into the gondola and the Goliath was truly a revelation in luxury.

Blatz was enthusiastic in his praise of the great machine and Andy was forced to admit to himself that his earlier suspicions appeared unfounded. He relaxed his vigilance somewhat and the secret agent of the Gerka sensed this change in the assistant pilot's attitude. Between them a real friendship started to develop and it was only natural that Bert and Harry were included in this feeling of comradeship.

On more than one occasion Blatz proved his sound technical knowledge, which could have been gained only at Friedrichshafen, a fact which influenced Andy in quieting his suspicions. In addition, there had been no report from the Washington headquarters of the secret service and it appeared that Blatz's record was all right.

Shipments of helium, the life-blood of the Goliath, were arriving daily from the Texas gas fields. The long, narrow cylinders were stacked in rows outside the hangar. When needed they would be trucked inside, the valves opened, and their contents would flow into the gas cells inside the duralumin hull. In this respect the United States led all the other nations in its precious supply of helium, a non-inflammable gas. Some of the Europeans were forced to use hydrogen, a highly inflammable gas, the use of which had resulted in some of the major dirigible catastrophes.

Work on the Goliath was well ahead of schedule and when Bert and Harry finished their work on the radio equipment, Harry announced that it would be necessary for him to return to Brooklyn at once for a final test of the equipment of the Neptune.

The submarine was to leave soon and Andy and Bert obtained leave to accompany Harry on his return east. When Blatz heard of the plans, he asked permission to accompany them. It would give him an opportunity to visit the American headquarters of the Gerka in New York.

"You might just as well make it a real holiday," Andy's father said when apprised of their plans. "One of our cabin monoplanes will be in tomorrow and I'll see that you are given the use of it for a week. Then you can fly east together."

The suggestion appealed to them and they accepted with enthusiasm. Two days later they were ready to depart. After stowing their luggage into the baggage compartment of the trim, fast National Airways monoplane, they each took farewell looks at the Goliath and then climbed into their places.

Andy was at the controls with Blatz in the seat beside him. Bert and Harry were sprawled in comfortable wicker chairs to the rear. The plane skimmed across the field and took off in a steep climb, circled the field once, and then headed northeast in a bee-line for New York.

The mountains, their crests covered with the fresh green of early spring foliage, reared their misty heads to the east. They would cut diagonally across them and Andy held the stick back and watched the altimeter climb. At five thousand he leveled off and settled down to the trip. They had plenty of gas to make it on one long hop.

Blatz was enjoying the trip, the rolling country beneath, the mountains which they were approaching and even the thrill of being in the air, which never grew old to him. His eyes sparkled and there was a bright glow to his cheeks. He'd like to get his hands on the controls and see how this American commercial job handled.

An hour later Andy turned to Blatz.

"Ever handled a ship like this?" he asked.

"I've done a little flying," admitted the European.

"Think you could handle it?"

Blatz nodded eagerly and Andy slipped out from behind the controls which the other took over.

Andy watched him keenly and noticed that Blatz settled into his chair like a veteran. His touch on the controls was firm but light and, unlike the beginner, he did not over-control.

The air over the mountains was rougher and Andy wondered how Blatz would come through. His question was soon answered. A down draft swirled them downward three hundred feet in the twinkling of an eye. A novice would have been panic-stricken, but Blatz gave her the gun and flipped out of it nicely.

"Good work," said Andy.

"More luck than anything else," was the reply, but Andy was very much inclined to disagree. There was no question in his mind now. Blatz was not only a good dirigible man but he was an expert flyer as well. The long-allayed suspicions Andy had harbored in the first weeks the civilian observer had been at Bellevue were re-awakened. He would communicate his distrust to Bert and Harry when they had a chance to talk alone. Until now he had kept his misgivings to himself but he felt that it was time the others knew how he felt.

They lunched over eastern Pennsylvania with the plane clipping the miles off at 110 an hour. Sandwiches had been brought in a liberal supply but the cool air had whetted their appetites and the basket of lunch soon disappeared.

"Oh, boy," said Bert. "Wait until I get to New York and sink my teeth in a big, juicy steak. Honestly, I'm almost starved. Those sandwiches were just teasers."

"How long before we'll be in?" asked Harry, who likewise confessed that the lunch had not satisfied his hunger.

"Another hour," replied Andy, who was back at the controls. "Next time we'll bring a restaurant along. From the way you fellows complain someone might get the idea you'd been working this morning."

Fifty-five minutes later they dipped over the National Airways field on the Jersey side and Andy nosed down to land. Blatz touched his arm.

"If Bert and Harry won't starve for five more minutes," he said, "I'd like to see New York from the air."

"We'll manage to hold out another few minutes," conceded the hungry pair, and Andy headed the monoplane east across the Jersey flats.

They dipped a wing in salute as the Statue of Liberty was passed and climbed steeply as they approached the Battery. On up town they sped over the canyons between the skyscrapers where hurrying crowds of shoppers were thronging the streets. The Empire State's gleaming tower was ahead, then beside, and then behind them. The Chrysler spire glittered in the sun and they looked down on the crowds in Times Square. Central Park was a fleeting panorama. Then they were over the Hudson, back to Jersey and sliding down out of the skyway with motor idling. They touched gently and rolled to a landing in front of the main control station where the number of their plane was taken and they were assigned to a hangar. Andy taxied the monoplane down the line to the No. 5 hangar where mechanics were ready to take it in charge.

"How did you like your aerial view of New York?" Andy asked Blatz.

"It was marvelous, breath-taking," laughed the other. "In Europe we have no city to compare with it. Your buildings; they go into the clouds."

"I'll say," replied Harry. "I've been on the Empire State tower when the clouds were so thick you couldn't see the street."

They entered the main administration building at the airport, cleaned up, and then took a taxi for New York. Through Jersey City and under the Hudson they went in the Holland Tubes and then through the maze of mid-afternoon traffic to their hotel just off Times Square.

While Andy was registering for the party, Bert saw the sign above the door of the grillroom, and, with a "See you later," departed to order the steak he had promised himself.

Andy, Blatz and Harry went up to their rooms, assured themselves that the double quarters were satisfactory, and then went down to join Bert in the grill.

"I ordered steaks for everyone," said the radio operator of the Goliath. "Anyone have any objections?"

There was no vocal protest and the steaks were placed before them a minute later.

"I've got to go over to the shipyard and report that I'm in town," said Harry. "Anyone like to run over to Brooklyn now and see what the Neptune looks like?"

"Count me in," replied Bert. "I want to see what kind of a tin can you're going to use in your attempt to reach the North Pole."

"How about you two?" asked Harry, turning to Andy and Blatz.

"I'll be glad to go in the morning," said Blatz, "but just now I'm a little tired. I'll stay here at the hotel, rest a while, and then perhaps stroll out and look around the city a bit."

"You'll have to count me out, too," said Andy. "I've a few errands that must be attended to and the sooner they are out of the way the more time I'll have to spend over at the shipyard."

Harry and Bert departed, after promising that they would return early in the evening so they could enjoy a show together. Blatz went up to their double room and Andy sat down at a writing desk to pen several important notes. He had been writing not more than five minutes when he looked up and saw a familiar figure going through the main doorway. He recognized the German civilian observer. But Blatz had just said that he was tired and was going to his room to rest?

Without waiting to ponder the question, Andy picked up the note he had been writing, stuffed it in his pocket, and hurried toward the entrance.

It was late afternoon and dusk had settled but he reached the street just in time to see Blatz step into a cab. There was something furtive, mysterious in the other's manner and Andy decided to follow. He motioned for a cab cruising by to stop. The driver was an alert, keen looking fellow and he responded instantly when Andy spoke to him.

"Keep that cab ahead in sight," said Andy, "and there's an extra five for you."

Gears meshed harshly as the cab lurched ahead and Andy started on one of the strangest adventures of his life.

CHAPTER IX
On the East Side

Lieutenant Larko, or Blatz as he was known to his American friends, wanted to get his visit to the American headquarters of the Gerka over as soon as possible. He did not look forward to it with pleasure and was anxious to return to his friends. The deeper he got into the intrigue the less he liked the mission which had been assigned to him by the dictator of Rubania.

On leaving the hotel, he sank back in the cushions of the taxicab and marveled at the dexterity of the driver, who guided his car between the moving streams of traffic with amazing skill. They worked away from the mid-town section, getting over on the east side where the streets were narrower, the lights dimmer and the pavement rough and bumpy.

Occasionally the gleam of the headlights of another car flashed in the mirror over the driver's head, but Blatz thought nothing of it until the driver leaned back as he slowed for a turn.

"There's another cab been following us ever since we left the hotel," he said. "Want me to try and shake them?"

"Not right now," replied Blatz. "Keep going; I'll watch them."

He turned and looked out the rear window. There was no mistake on the part of the driver; another machine was following, making every turn they did, maintaining the same speed and keeping about a block to the rear. Had the American secret service become suspicious of him and placed him under surveillance?

The thought alarmed Blatz and he ordered the driver to attempt to lose the pursuing machine. For fifteen minutes they turned and twisted from one street to another, darted through alleys and doubled back onto thoroughfares. At last the lights of the other machine vanished and Blatz felt sure that they had lost their pursuers.

He gave the order to continue to the address he had given the driver and relaxed again. He would be glad to get back to the hotel and rejoin his friends.

The American headquarters of the Gerka were located on the fifth floor of a warehouse building on the east side, a district which was anything but reassuring after dusk had fallen. Street lights cast their feeble rays at infrequent intervals and there was no traffic on the street. One dusty electric globe hung in the little cubby which was marked "watchman's office."

"Want me to wait?" asked the taxi driver.

"That's not necessary," replied Blatz. "I'll call a cab when I'm ready to return."

The taxi lurched down the street and Blatz walked up to the watchman's window.

The password of the Gerka was in Rubanian and Blatz spoke a guttural phrase.

The watchman, a middle aged man with distinct Rubanian features, stepped to a phone and made sure that Blatz was really an agent of the Gerka. Informed that the newcomer was to be shown to the headquarters, he took Blatz into the dim confines of the building and showed him into a freight elevator. They were lifted slowly to the fifth floor and when the door opened, Blatz stepped out into a comfortably furnished suite of rooms.

A secretary took his number and mission and five minutes later he was ushered into the inner chamber, to face Lothar Vendra, head of the American branch of the Gerka.

Vendra was an impressive individual. He was tall, broad-shouldered, and handsome in a bitter sort of way.

"I am most happy to greet you," he told Blatz, extending his hand in welcome.

"I am happy to be here," replied Blatz, with an enthusiasm that he did not honestly feel.

"Sit down," motioned Vendra, "and tell me all that has happened since you arrived at Bellevue and how you happen to be in New York at this time."

Blatz recounted in detail the events that had taken place since he had arrived at the home of the Goliath. When he mentioned the name of Boris Dubra, the mechanic who had been wounded in his attempt to damage the Goliath's hangar, Vendra's face clouded with anger.

"I had heard of that," he said. "Dubra was a fool. We are just as well off without him. You will be able to accomplish the task alone."

"I'm not so sure that I will fulfill my mission," replied Blatz.

"What's that?" demanded Vendra.

"I have a feeling that the Americans, especially Andy High, are suspicious," explained Blatz. "When I left the hotel a few minutes ago I was followed and only by the amazing dexterity of my taxi driver was I able to elude my pursuer."

"You must have been mistaken," insisted Vendra. "Your papers are in perfect order."

"I was not mistaken," said Blatz, clearly and decisively. "Every precaution must be taken or I will find myself in an American military prison."

"I agree that you must be careful," admitted Vendra, "but His Excellency is most anxious that the Goliath be destroyed at once. In his latest communication he especially stressed this point. This air monster must never become the king of the skies!"

The words came to Blatz through a mist of memories. He could see the silver sides of the Goliath as the great ship lay in its hangar, hear the tap of hammers and cries of the workmen as they rushed it to completion, see the pride and joy in Andy's eyes as the young engineer looked at the great skycraft he had helped to create. And his job was to destroy all this. The airman in him rebelled and Vendra, sensing the emotional conflict, moved closer.

"Remember," he warned. "You are a Rubanian, a member of the Gerka, who is pledged to duty even unto death!"

Blatz nodded dismally. There was no getting away from the facts. He would have to destroy the Goliath.

"You may inform His Excellency," he said, "that I will do my best."

He was about to leave when a buzzer rang sharply. Vendra seized the telephone and a look of alarm came over his face.

"There's trouble down at the entrance," he said. "The watchman just found a man prowling around. He knocked him out and is bringing him up here."

Andy's pursuit of the German observer had not been successful for his driver had finally lost the cab in the maze of quick turns Blatz's driver had made after being ordered to shake off pursuit.

But Andy was not easily discouraged and he ordered his own taxi to return to the street on which they had been when Blatz had started his zig-zig tactics. There was a possibility that the cab he sought might return and continue its journey from that point. His hunch was correct and within ten minutes the machine he had lost rolled down the street. This time his driver put out his lights and they followed, Andy in the meantime having agreed to fend off any police charges that might be brought for running without lights.

He was less than two hundred yards away when Blatz entered the warehouse and Andy was slipping into the building when the night watchman returned and caught him.

The challenge was in Rubanian, a language unfamiliar to Andy. He replied in American, explaining that he was looking for a friend who was to meet him at that address.

The explanation failed to satisfy the watchman, who ordered Andy out. The watchman was too anxious to get rid of him and Andy refused to leave. The attack followed almost instantly, and the burly watchman hurled himself at the slender airman with surprising speed.

Taken unaware, Andy went down in a heap. He struggled to his feet and turned to face the next rush by the watchman. He partially fended off the first blow but another, starting low and coming up with tremendous force, caught him on the point of the chin. His knees wobbled, a mist clouded his eyes, his mouth was strangely dry and he had a sensation of falling from a great height. Then a curtain of darkness descended.

The watchman picked him up carried him into the elevator, and finally walked into Vendra's office with the unconscious Andy in his arms.

Blatz started back in white-faced amazement.

"Is he badly hurt?" he asked.

"No," grunted the watchman. "He'll come around in a few minutes. He struck his head against a door sill when I knocked him down."

"This is terrible," said Blatz. "Now Andy's suspicions of me will be confirmed. It will be no use for me to return to Bellevue after this."

"What do you mean?" asked Vendra.

"Just this," explained Blatz. "Your bulldog watchman here has knocked out Andy High, son of Charles High, executive vice president of the National Airways who is in charge of the building of the Goliath. Andy is my 'chaperon' at Bellevue and the only one who has appeared to be suspicious of me. He must have followed me from the hotel."

Vendra was silent for a minute, pondering the situation which confronted them.

"It is regrettable," he said. "You must return to Bellevue to fulfill your mission of destroying the Goliath, the air monster."

"But I can't go back now," protested Blatz.

"Return to your hotel at once," said Vendra.

"When anyone asks where you have been, tell them on a long taxi ride through the city and Central Park."

"Andy will never believe such a story," protested Blatz.

"He won't be able to disprove it," countered Vendra. "As soon as you leave I'll take him out of here. We'll leave him in another street before he recovers consciousness. He'll never be able to find his way back here and you'll make a complete denial if he ever openly accuses you. It is ticklish, I admit, but it is the only way out."

Blatz finally agreed and hastened from the room, to return at once to the hotel where he found Bert and Harry waiting.

"Where's Andy?" asked Bert.

"I don't know," replied Blatz. "I've been on a long taxi ride." Which, he told himself, was quite true.

An hour later Andy arrived in a cab, his clothes so dirty and disheveled that he attracted open attention as he walked through the fashionable lobby of the hotel. The clerks eyed him with disgust but they dared not protest at his appearance. When he appeared in his room, he was greeted with exclamations of astonishment.

"What under the sun happened to you?" asked Bert. "Did a taxi walk all over you?"

"Something, hit me," said Andy, "while I was down on the east side. The next thing I knew I was lying in a street and a policeman was shaking me. I finally convinced him that I was sane and sober, and he let me come back here. I haven't figured it out just yet; my head's too dizzy."

He looked straight at Blatz when he added:

"But I have a hunch I'll get it straight when I get over this headache."

CHAPTER X
The Neptune Sails

Andy was shaky from his experience over on the east side and while Bert, Harry and Blatz went out to a show, he remained at the hotel to rest and think things over.

He was positive that he had seen Blatz go into the warehouse and the conviction grew that the German civilian observer was not all that he claimed to be. Andy felt a crisis coming, something he couldn't exactly put into words, but a vague feeling that trouble was just around the corner. He was asleep when the others returned at midnight from the theater and they did not waken him.

Andy felt much refreshed the next morning and they decided to accompany Harry on his visit to the shipyard.

"It's the finest tin fish I've ever seen," said Bert, who had visited the Neptune the afternoon before. "They've got just about everything they need in it."

"It is a wonderful boat," admitted Harry proudly, "but I'll have to confess that traveling in the Neptune won't be able to compare with the Goliath. When we're submerged the air isn't any too good if we're down three or four hours and we're pretty cramped for space."

"Let's get under way," said Andy. "I'm anxious to see this wonderful tin fish."

They took a taxi across town, rolled over the Brooklyn bridge and fifteen minutes later were walking into the shipyard where the Neptune was being groomed for its polar trip.

The submarine was lying beside a stubby wharf with its main hatch open. Workmen were busy passing supplies down into its depths as Andy and his party arrived.

"My gosh," exclaimed Andy. "I didn't suppose you had a submarine of this type. It's almost as big as one of the navy's super-cruisers."

"Just about," agreed Harry. "As a matter-of-fact, this sub was built for naval purposes by the Seabright yards. They used it as a demonstrator in selling similar models to South American navies. It has just about every modern gadget on it that inventors could devise. As a result of this working model, the Seabright people landed contracts for about 25 million in work. The Neptune had served its purpose and they were willing to sell it to Gilbert Mathews at a very reasonable figure when he started looking for a ship in which to make the polar trip. The Seabright engineers have made all of the necessary changes for polar cruising and have just put their official approval on the Neptune, which means we'll be starting north within a few days."

"I'd like to see inside the Neptune," said Blatz, adding, "I've never been in a submarine before."

"All right," agreed Harry, "but we'll have to keep out of the way of the crew bringing in stores Let's go."

They scrambled down the ladder and reached the rivet-studded deck of the Neptune. There was a lull in the steady stream of boxes being carried into the interior and they hurried through the main hatch and into the conning tower, then down into the main control room.

Andy looked about in amazement at the compactness of the instruments in the "brains" of the submarine. There was not an inch of waste space in the spotlessly white interior of the steel fish.

Harry led them through the forward engine room and into the crew quarters where double-decked bunks lined the walls. Just ahead were the officers' quarters, slightly better furnished than those of the crew and beyond this was the radio cubby where Harry would practically live from the time they left the Brooklyn shipyard until they returned from the desolate ice wastes of the far north.

They went on ahead into the room usually used as a torpedo room. This had been fitted with scientific equipment for sounding the ocean depths, and determining the material at the bottom of the Arctic. In addition to the scientific paraphernalia, the forward room contained the all important rescue chambers. In this room was located the powerful drill which was capable of boring fifty feet upward straight through the ice, opening a tunnel large enough for a man to wriggle through in case the submarine became trapped by ice. There was also an escape passage through the forward torpedo tubes.

The inspection of the forward half of the sub completed, they turned to the after quarters. Another large engine room was located after the main control room and beyond this was another room with double-decked bunks while just back of that was the galley.

"You've got a place to cook food," said Bert, "but where do you eat?"

"Just about any place we find convenient," replied Harry. "There are a number of folding tables that can be pulled out in the crews' quarters but if the going is rough or we're busy, we take on food when and where we can get it."

"When you're pitching around on the North Atlantic and trying to connect a little food with that hungry mouth of yours, just remember what a pleasant time I'll be having on the Goliath where there's plenty of room to stretch and plenty of room to eat," said Bert.

"I'll probably remember that a good many times," grinned Harry, "but if you radio me a description of some of those nice meals of yours. I'll refuse to answer."

They completed their inspection of the Neptune and had climbed back to the wharf when a roadster rolled through the shipyard gate.

"Just a minute, fellows," said Harry. "Here comes Gilbert Mathews. I'd like to have you meet him."

The commander of the Neptune was tall and broad-shouldered. His walk was vigorous and he was hatless.

His brown hair was slightly gray at the temples and he might be anywhere from 35 to 45 years old.

"Hello, Harry," he said as he came up. "Your radio equipment all ready?"

"Everything's tested and in fine shape," replied the radio operator. "I'd like to have you meet my friends."

"Delighted," said the explorer, and he greeted Blatz, Bert and Andy cordially.

"I've had some very pleasant conferences with your father," he told Andy. "Will we meet at the North pole this summer?"

"I sincerely hope so," replied Andy. "Bert is chief radio operator on the Goliath and I will make the trip as assistant to Captain Harkins."

"Then I am sure that we will meet again," replied Mathews. He turned to Harry.

"Did the orders reach you at your hotel before you left this morning?" he asked.

"No sir," replied Harry.

"Then this will come as somewhat of a surprise," smiled Mathews. "We'll leave at sunrise and every member of the crew has been ordered on board tonight."

"It certainly is a surprise," gasped Harry, "but I'll be aboard ship tonight."

"You're leaving almost two weeks earlier than you had first planned," said Andy.

"Conditions in the Arctic are more open than they have been for a number of years," replied the explorer, "and I am anxious to get the Neptune into the ice as soon as possible."

"We probably will not see you again," said Andy, "but we wish you every good fortune and we'll see you at the North pole."

"Thank you for your good wishes," replied Mathews. "In return, I wish the Goliath a fair voyage and a fast one."

The explorer left them and hurried down the ladder to supervise the final preparations for the departure of the Neptune.

Harry was busy the remainder of the day, finishing the task of getting his kit together and sending goodbye telegrams to relatives, for his parents lived in Illinois and would not be able to reach New York before sailing time.

Hotel reporters learned that the assistant pilot of the Goliath was in the city and when they returned to the hotel in late afternoon, half a dozen were waiting for Andy.

They plied him with questions. How long would it be before the Goliath was ready to take the air; what would the big ship do; where would it go on its trial flights; was it true that attempts had been made to destroy the ship in its hangar; when would it start on the cruise into the Arctic regions?

To all these questions Andy was able to give only the most general of answers for he was bound in secrecy not to reveal definite information about the Goliath or the plans for its trial flights. Andy and his friends posed while flashlights flared but finally they were alone in their rooms.

Harry had finished the score of small tasks which had been necessary when the final sail order, was given and he stretched out on one of the beds, his hands clasped above his head.

"Tonight we're all here together," he said. "Tomorrow I'll be going down the sound in the tin fish; next week you'll be aloft as the Goliath tries its wings, and the next time we meet will be at the North pole. Believe me, that's adventure."

"How I envy you all," said Blatz, his voice low and earnest, and Andy actually felt sorry for the European whom he had come to firmly suspicion. If he could wipe those doubts out of his mind, he would thoroughly like Blatz for the foreigner was a born airman and would be a real asset to the technical staff of National Airways.

"When you sail away for the North pole in the Goliath," he told Andy, "I'll stay on the ground at Bellevue and watch you fade into the north but I'll glory with you in success."

"I'm hungry," announced Bert. "Let's go down and get something to eat. If we sit around here we'll all get blue for we're going to miss Harry a lot. There's just this one consolation. We'll be able to talk back and forth daily on our low wave sets unless the Arctic puts up a wall of static we can't break through."

Their last meal together was a quiet affair despite Bert's efforts to make it jolly and cheerful. With Harry going aboard ship within the next hour or so and the

Neptune casting off at dawn, they knew the start of the great adventure was at hand and it awed them all.

A messenger paged Harry in the dining room and handed him a telegram. The Neptune's radio operator tore it open with fingers that shook just a little and read it hungrily. His face whitened for a moment and he folded the message carefully and placed it in an inner pocket. There was a suspicion of a tear in one eye.

"A wire from Dad and Mother," he said. "They're the best ever."

An hour later they stepped out of a taxi on the Brooklyn wharf. Lights glowed over the Neptune; cars hurried up to disgorge other members of the crew, newspaper men were buzzing around, flashlights blazed and over the whole scene there was a feeling of tension.

Gilbert Mathews was at the head of the ladder, checking in every man as he came aboard. Harry reported and was checked off the list. He turned to his friends from Bellevue.

"I can't say very much," he told them. "Everything is sort of choked up in my throat. Bert, old scout, I'll be tuning up for your messages. Don't forget me."

"I won't," promised the Goliath's operator.

"So long, fellows," said Harry and he turned and hastened down the ladder to the deck of the Neptune. He paused for a moment and waved before stepping inside the steel hull.

When they returned to their hotel, Blatz stopped at a newsstand to buy an early edition of one of the morning papers. They were so much more comprehensive than the Rubanian papers to which he had been accustomed and he thoroughly enjoyed reading them. In the quiet of his room he digested the news of the day. A story on an inside page caught and held his attention. The dateline was "KRATZ, Rubania." The story told of the growing unrest against the regime of Dictator Reikoff, adding that this bad feeling was centered in the powerful air corps, the largest unit of the Rubanian army.

Blatz knew what they meant. Reikoff had been making unjust demands of his airmen and he was sitting on an open powder keg which was likely to explode with disastrous results to himself. Blatz almost wished that revolution would sweep the country and rid Rubania of its dictator. He was thoroughly disgusted and out of sympathy with the task to which he had been assigned, that of destroying the Goliath, and he would welcome any opportunity to escape but as long as Reikoff lived and ruled it would mean death for Blatz if he failed to carry out his mission.

Andy stepped through the door which connected the double room.

"Any objections to our returning to Bellevue in the morning?" he asked.

"No, why?" replied Blatz.

"Oh, there's no reason for us to stay on longer here but I thought you might have some business over on the east side to transact."

Andy's keen eyes were watching Blatz's face, searching for some change of expression that would indicate his alarm. There was none; the civilian observer outwardly appeared cool and unruffled but it was well that Andy could not see the flash of fear that seared across his mind. It was true, then, that Andy did suspect him. He was warning him in this way to watch his step. Undoubtedly he would tell the secret service. If he, Blatz, were to accomplish his mission of destruction it must be immediately after his return to Bellevue.

"There is nothing to keep me in the city," replied Blatz, "and I am anxious to get back and see the finishing touches put on the Goliath."

"Then we'll get an early start," said Andy, "drop down the harbor and say goodbye to the Neptune and then head for home. We ought to be there in time for lunch."

They were up shortly after dawn but it was eight o'clock by the time they reached the airport of the National Airways in Jersey, had stowed their baggage in the monoplane and were ready to take the air. Andy took over the controls, Blatz climbed in beside him and Bert stowed his more ample bulk in a chair just behind and beside a window where he could wave when they passed the Neptune.

Satisfied that the motor of the monoplane was functioning perfectly, Andy sent the plane speeding over the crushed rock runway and into the slanting rays of the sun. He circled the field until he had plenty of altitude, and then cut across the Jersey flats where the blue Atlantic gleamed in the distance.

The Neptune must have started at the crack of dawn, for the submarine was far down the bay when they finally picked it up. The Neptune was running on the surface at ten knots an hour, its sharp nose cleaving through the sparkling waves and its decks almost awash. The main hatch was open and half a dozen of the crew were on top of the conning tower.

Andy sent the monoplane down in a gentle glide, levelled off, and skimmed over the water with motor on full. They flashed past the Neptune, raced out to sea, turned and roared back: Someone on the conning tower was waving frantically.

The three in the monoplane caught a fleeting glimpse of Harry as they sped past. The Neptune was off, headed for Plymouth, England, on the first leg of its long and adventurous trip into the Arctic.

CHAPTER XI
In The Hangar

The return flight to Bellevue was uneventful and the monoplane settled down beside the Goliath's hangar shortly after noon. Andy taxied the plane up to the apron and they piled out and hurried into the main hangar to see what progress had been made on the Goliath since their departure.

Even in the short time they had been away the crews had put on the finishing touches. The great silver hull gleamed in the softened light of the hangar. The main gondola had been completed, the observation cockpits on top of the big bag were in place and hundreds of helium tanks were piled along the walls of the hangar—empty. That meant that the gas cells had been filled with the precious gas. The Goliath was almost ready to take the air.

Charles High and Captain Harkins hurried up to them.

"How does the Goliath look today?" Andy's father asked.

"Wonderful, Dad, simply wonderful," replied Andy. "When will you make the first test?"

"We may walk it out of the hangar tomorrow but we won't make a real flight for several days," replied the vice president in charge of operations for the National Airways. "The army has a finger in the pie and when we actually take the air several members of the general staff and a dozen air corps experts will want to be aboard to see if it behaves to specifications."

"I'm sure it will," put in Blatz. "I've seen a good many of Doctor Eckener's ships at Friedrichshafen and with all due respect to the Herr Doctor, the Goliath is the finest, most carefully designed and built aircraft I have ever seen."

"That's a real compliment," chuckled Bert. "It isn't very often a European will concede superiority to an American in anything."

"Blatz is right," said Captain Harkins quietly. "There is no question about the Goliath being the finest airship ever built. I expect it to live up to our every hope in its performance in the air."

"We were surprised when Gilbert Mathews informed Harry of the advance in sailing plans," Andy told his father.

"I was a trifle surprised, too," admitted the vice president of National Airways. "Mathews wired me the same day of the change in plans and I replied that the Goliath would be able to advance its air tests and keep the date to meet him at the pole even with the earlier sailing. I can't blame him, though, for wanting to take advantage of the favorable ice conditions which are reported in the north now."

"The Neptune is a great submarine," said Bert, "as far as subs go but I'll take an airplane or dirigible any day. Being shut up in one of those things is like sailing around in a tub. I wouldn't trade my radio cubby on the Goliath for a dozen jobs on the Neptune."

"Someone had to go on the Neptune and we'll give Harry plenty of credit for his nerve," said Andy. "Will you be able to pick up his message tonight?"

"I promised him I'd tune in every night at eight," replied Bert. "We ought to hear him plainly."

Captain Harkins asked Andy to accompany him to the main office to check over the final construction reports on the Goliath while Andy's father took Blatz on an inspection trip over the big bag. They entered the luxuriously furnished gondola with its lounge and radio room, the dining salon and the glass enclosed promenade. Then to the upper deck of the gondola where the passenger cabins were located. The interior finish was in a cool, pleasing gray, a favorable contrast to the silver of the metalized hull.

After leaving the gondola, they walked down the main runway which was built lengthwise down the middle of the Goliath. In the earlier dirigibles this had been little more than a catwalk and none too safe. A plunge off would have meant crashing through the outer fabric and a fall to earth. In the Goliath the main runway was a substantial affair six feet wide. Made of duralumin, it was strong but light and guard rails proved ample protection for members of the crew or passengers who might be permitted to view the interior of the big airship.

The gas bags were inflated with, helium and held rigidly in place, six of them in the forward part of the ship and six of them in the after section. The transverse rings built of girders of duralumin separated each bag and there was a narrow catwalk between each large gas cell to facilitate the stopping of any possible leaks.

The motor gondolas were built inside the hull with the flexible propeller shafts sticking through the side. There were six of the motor gondolas on each side and each car was carefully insulated so that fire could be confined to one section of the dirigible.

The mid-section of the Goliath was forbidden ground to Blatz for it was here that space had been provided for the storing of airplanes in time of war. A special device which hooked onto the planes while they were in flight and lifted them into the hold in the center of the airship had been perfected by Captain Harkins and Blatz was anxious to see this. He was in for a disappointment that afternoon for Charles High did not take him back that far. Instead, they stopped at the fourth transverse girder where a stairway led to the top of the dirigible. There were six of these stairs all told, each running to the top and giving access to the observation cockpits. There was a runway on top of the Goliath with strong cables stretched along the side but it would be almost worth a man's life to attempt to walk on it while the dirigible was in motion and especially if the air happened to be the least bit rough. A fine place, thought Blatz, for anyone who was inclined to be seasick.

They walked along the outer runway toward the rear of the Goliath and from this elevation Blatz had a real opportunity to realize the size of the new king of the air— the craft which Reikoff had termed an "air monster." When they reached the after part of the dirigible with its great fin and elevators, they descended into the interior. Motor crews were busy tuning up the engines and the air was filled with the tenseness of preparation.

At dinner that night Captain Harkins announced that he had received word from the army air corps that the officers who would report on the trial flights of the Goliath would be at Bellevue before noon the next day.

"That means we'll walk the Goliath out at one o'clock if the wind and weather are favorable."

The words came to Blatz through a daze. He had seen Andy and Merritt Timms of the secret service conferring before dinner and from the look Timms had shot his way he knew that he had been the object of their discussion. The Goliath would be out of its hangar tomorrow. Army officers would arrive and from then on there would be little opportunity to damage the big ship. Tonight was the time! Even though Andy might be suspicious, he would hardly believe him capable of so daring an attempt on the Goliath. Blatz set his jaw firmly. It was going to be a task he did not fancy for his love for the Goliath had grown until he quailed at the thought of its destruction. But he was a Rubanian, a member of the Gerka. He could not escape from his duty.

Andy found an item of interest in the evening paper which he showed Blatz. It was another bulletin from Rubania. Revolution was threatening. Reikoff's power was tottering.

Blatz read it eagerly. Perhaps he would not be forced to destroy the Goliath after all. If he could only wait a few more days. But the one big opportunity was at hand. Tonight was the logical one for his task.

Andy noticed the European's hands shook as he read the item, but Blatz's face showed no change of emotion.

"Come on, you two," called Bert. "Let's get over to my radio shack and we'll see if we can pick up Harry somewhere off Long Island in his tin fish."

It was nearly eight o'clock when they reached the radio shack just outside the main hangar and it took Bert some time to time up his apparatus. He plugged in on the main transmitter and a minute later turned around with a grin.

"Harry is burning up the air," chuckled Bert. "I was late coming in and wants to know what I'd been doing. Accuses me of over-eating. Imagine."

The stream of dots and dashes which had been flickering through the air ceased.

"We're going to try the radiophone now," explained Bert, "and we'll be able to talk back and forth."

When Bert completed the proper adjustments Andy almost fell out of his chair as Harry's voice echoed in the little room.

"Hello Bert. Hello Andy," said Harry, eight hundred miles away and under water in the radio room of the Neptune. "Tell Blatz hello, too, if he's with you," added Harry.

"The three of us are in the radio shack," replied Bert, "and I resent your implication that I overate tonight. I over-talked."

"Which is just as bad," came back the voice over the ether waves.

Andy picked up the microphone and spoke to Harry.

"How is the trip going?" he asked, "and where are you?"

"We're about 130 miles out of New York harbor," replied Harry. "The sea is a little choppy but nothing to write home about. Everything is running smoothly so far and we ought to put in at Plymouth in about 12 days."

"How's the air in your tin fish?" Bert wanted to know.

"Fine," replied Harry. "The main hatch has been open all of the time and I haven't a thing to complain about. I'll have to sign off now and send some messages for Mr. Mathews. I'll buzz you again at eight in the morning."

"Be sure you make it at eight o'clock our time," warned Bert as he signed off.

Bert had some work to do on his reserve radio equipment and Andy went to his own office to look over the correspondence which had accumulated during his absence in New York.

Blatz, professing to be tired after the flight down from New York, said he would go to the hotel and retire early. Andy watched until the German civilian observer bad crossed the track and was well on his way to the hotel. He had told Timms of his experience in New York but the secret service man was still inclined not to doubt Blatz's right to be at Bellevue. Whatever watching of the observer was done would have to be by Andy.

The assistant pilot of the Goliath was busy half an hour reading and sorting the mail. It was unusually quiet around the hangar that night so the scuffing of something against a stick caught Andy's attention. Someone was walking cautiously toward the hangar!

Andy remained in his chair, fingering through the pile of letters before him. The guarded sound came again. At the end of a minute he turned out the light and slipped out of his office. A small door which led into the main hangar was open.

Andy returned to his office to get his flashlight. Remembering that he had left it at the hotel, he found some matches beside a half dozen red lanterns which were used to mark danger places on the field. Since the Goliath used helium there was no danger of an explosion from striking a match in the hangar or, for that matter, aboard the Goliath itself.

The assistant pilot of the dirigible stepped quickly through the door and paused to accustom his eyes to the heavy darkness of the interior. He slipped off his shoes and then moved slowly toward the lighter outline of the silvered hull of the Goliath.

Andy paused. Someone was moving slowly just ahead of him. The young airman groped his way ahead, hands outstretched. The next second he was clutching someone's coat.

They came to grips, but only for a second. The unknown invader of the hangar slipped out of his coat and Andy heard him running out of the hangar.

Muttering to himself in disgust, Andy stooped to strike a match and look at the coat he had seized. As he struck a match, he slipped and stumbled headlong. The match dropped into a chunk of oily waste. It flared and burst into flame but Andy remained motionless on the floor, his head resting against a heavy wood block it had struck.

The fire in the waste glowed brightly and leaped higher as it fed on the oil which saturated the waste. Unless help reached Andy soon the fire would spread to other parts of the hangar and the Goliath itself would be in danger of destruction!

CHAPTER XII
Trial Flight

While Andy lay senseless on the floor of the hangar with the flames from the oil-soaked waste mounting higher, a shadow appeared in the doorway. It was Blatz, whom Andy had surprised in the hangar as he was about to attempt the destruction of the Goliath.

The German observer crept closer to the flames and it was not until he was almost at the blaze that he discerned the inert form of the assistant pilot.

"Andy," he cried, "Andy!"

There was no answer and Blatz acted with sudden determination. He picked up the coat which Andy still clutched and used the garment to beat out the flames. That task accomplished he turned on his flashlight and bent down to examine the lump on Andy's forehead. The young airman groaned and Blatz chuckled grimly. The game was nearly over. He was glad.

He managed to pick Andy up and carried the now half-conscious American out of the hangar and into his office, where he turned on the light.

Andy came to several minutes later and finally focused his eyes long enough on one spot to see Blatz standing in front of him.

"I'm on to you," cried Andy, struggling to get out of his chair. "You're trying to destroy the Goliath."

"Easy, Andy, easy," urged Blatz. "You've had another nasty bump on your head. The Goliath is all right."

"The last I remember is falling," said Andy. "How did I get in here and what are you doing around the hangar at this time of night?"

"You took a tumble, all right," agreed Blatz, "and the match you had in your hand fell into a handful of greasy waste. You'd chased me out of the hangar but if I hadn't been curious when you failed to follow, the whole thing might have burned up. As it was, I got back in time to put out the fire before it got to you or the Goliath."

Andy looked at the speaker with incredulous eyes.

"If that's true," he said, "I have done you a great wrong."

Before the observer could reply, Bert burst through the door.

"Big news," he said. "The Rubanian air force rebelled this afternoon and forced Dictator Reikoff clear out of the country. I just got that bulletin over in the radio shack."

"You're sure there's no mistake?" asked Blatz.

"Positive," replied Bert. "It was an Associated Press dispatch broadcast through the courtesy of one of the Louisville papers."

Blatz looked at Andy and they smiled understanding.

"What's the joke," demanded Bert.

"There isn't any joke," replied Blatz gravely, "and I can now tell you the truth. I am Lieut. Serge Larko of the Rubanian air force. I was assigned to special duty as an agent of the Gerka, our secret police, and my mission was to make a non-stop flight to the United States, make my way to Bellevue and bring about the destruction of the Goliath."

Bert stared at him in speechless wonder but Andy nodded and said.

"Then you were piloting the gray monoplane we chased that afternoon?"

"Right," said Serge. "You gave me a real scare."

"And you went into that warehouse on the east side while we were in New York?" continued Andy.

"Right again."

"And tonight you went into the hangar for the purpose of destroying the Goliath?"

"I started in with that purpose," admitted Serge, "but I'm too much of an airman. After I got inside I couldn't bring myself to damage that beautiful craft. I was about to leave when you entered and we met in the dark. You know the rest of the story."

"I know that it was mighty fortunate for me that you came back," replied Andy and be grasped Serge warmly by the hand. "Now that the menace of Reikoff has been removed from your homeland, I'm sure we'll become real friends. We'll see Dad and Captain Harkins about having you added to the permanent staff of the National Airways."

"I'd like that," smiled Serge happily, "but they'll probably order me away from Bellevue or the secret service may take a hand in my case."

"I think Merritt Timms can be made to see things my way," replied Andy.

"When did you first suspect me?" asked Serge. "Almost as soon as you arrived," admitted Andy. "If you remember I questioned you about Friedrichshafen and suggested that you might know Karl Staab? When you admitted that you knew Staab I decided something was wrong for as far as I know Staab never existed outside of my own mind."

"But I really have been at Friedrichshafen," replied Serge.

"I believed that," said Andy, "for your technical knowledge showed you had been trained with the Germans. Now let's go over to the hotel and see Dad and Captain Harkins."

The conference at the hotel was interesting and successful and before the long evening drew to a close it was agreed that Serge Larko, who had assumed his real identity, should become a permanent member of the Goliath's crew.

Even though the next day promised to be unusually busy, it was midnight before they were in bed but they were up at the crack of dawn.

Serge was happier than he had been in months and Andy felt that a great weight had been lifted from his mind. There was no further danger to the Goliath from inside sources and they were practically ready for the test flights.

Lieut. Jim Crummit, in command of the army pursuit ships at Bellevue, stopped them as they left the hotel.

"Will you want us to stand by this afternoon in case you decide to take the Goliath aloft?" he asked Captain Harkins.

"I hardly think that will be necessary, Lieutenant!" replied the commander of the Goliath. "Any flight we might make would be confined to the limits of the field."

"Right, sir," said the army officer as he turned and walked toward the hangars which housed the army ships.

At eight o'clock Andy, Serge and Bert gathered in the radio shack and Bert turned his set to talk with the Neptune. There was a steady crackle of interference but

Bert stepped up the power with the hope that he would get through to the Neptune.

"Looks like we're out of luck this morning," he finally announced, "but I'll give it one more try." He turned to the dial again, tuning so carefully the black disks hardly moved.

"Harry's coming in now," he said. "I'll have it strong in a minute."

Bert switched over to the radiophone loudspeaker and the boys heard Harry calling, "Hello Bellevue. Good morning."

"Good morning yourself," replied Bert. "Have fish for breakfast?"

"Not this morning," replied Harry. "Besides, it's mid-forenoon out where we are. How's the Goliath?"

Andy picked up the microphone and told Harry briefly what had taken place the night before, adding that Serge had been added to the crew of the Goliath and would make the trip to the North pole.

"I'm glad to hear that," replied Harry over the magic waves which bridged the hundreds of miles between them. "I'll say hello to Serge if he'll take the mike now."

The young Rubanian conversed with Harry for several minutes and then the operator of the Neptune signed off.

"I'll be back on the air tonight at eight," he told Bert. "Be sure and let me know how the Goliath behaves on her first trip out of the hangar."

The interior of the great hangar was alive with activity that morning. Final weight checks were being made for the war department. Specifications on the total weight were very strict and builders of dirigibles were always prone to exceed the specification limit.

Captain Harkins and Andy's father were at first one end of the Goliath and then at the other supervising the countless last minute tasks.

A tri-motor droned over the field at 11 o'clock, circled and dropped down to waddle across the fresh green of the meadow. It stopped at one side of the Goliath's hangar and a dozen army officers, all with the wings of the air corps on their collars, descended and walked toward the hangar.

Captain Harkins and Andy's father hastened to make them welcome and assure them that the Goliath would be ready for a walk-out test immediately after lunch.

While the builders and chief engineers of the Goliath entertained the visiting army delegation at the hotel at noon, Andy and Serge made the final inspection of the big ship. The ground crew had been drilled in its task and the operator of the portable mooring mast to which the nose of the Goliath had been fastened had thoroughly rehearsed his part.

At one o'clock the army officers, accompanied by Captain Harkins and Charles High, returned from the hotel. For the next hour the army men went over the Goliath, inspecting every yard of fabric and testing every duralumin beam. Motors were put on test, Bert demonstrated the power of his radio equipment and even the passenger cabins came in for a rigid inspection.

At two o'clock Captain Harkins stepped into the control room at the forward end of the gondola.

"Everything ready?" he asked Andy, in whom he had placed a large share of responsibility for the successful flight.

"Everything ready, sir," replied Andy.

Captain Harkins took over the controls. The army officers lined the windows of the control room. Andy leaned out one window on the right side and placed a whistle to his mouth. He was wearing a telephone headset while on the wall of the control room was a compact little switchboard so that he could instantly communicate with any part of the dirigible whenever Captain Harkins gave a command.

The great moment was at hand. The Goliath was ready for its first test, the walk-out from the hangar. Months of work and planning were represented in the great ship; would it live up to expectations?

Andy sounded a shrill blast on the whistle. The ground crew, which had been waiting for the signal, leaped to its stations. The operator of the portable mooring mast started the engine of the big tractor-truck which carried the mast.

The assistant pilot of the Goliath looked at Captain Harkins, who nodded quietly.

Andy sounded two long blasts on the whistle. The shackles which had held the Goliath in the hangar for so many months were loosened. The great airship quivered slightly as though eager to test its power.

The blasts of the whistle echoed through the hangar and the operator of the huge tractor ahead eased in the clutch and started forward. The Goliath lurched slightly at the tug of the mooring mast, and then slowly started ahead. The ground crew steadied the great hulk as it was eased out of the shed. There was no wind and in ten minutes the Goliath was outside the hangar in which it had been born and in which it had grown to such proportions that it was king of all the skycraft.

The Goliath moved steadily ahead until it was well away from the hangar. Captain Harkins signaled Andy and another blast of the whistle stopped the portable mooring mast.

Captain Harkins conferred with the ranking air corps officer and Andy caught a snatch of their conversation. They were going to take the Goliath up. The big ship was behaving perfectly and the army men were anxious for an air test. Captain Harkins assented and turned to Andy.

"Have the motors started at once," he ordered.

Andy cut in a main phone connection so that he could talk to each of the 12 motor rooms at the same time.

"Start your motors," he said, "and stand by for flight."

Sharp, joyous answers echoed in his ears as the engineers hastened to start the engines which were capable of sending the Goliath through the air at a maximum speed of 120 miles an hour.

The rear engine crews were the first to get their motors turning over but within a minute the steady pulse of the 12 powerful engines could be heard. Engine room after engine room reported to Andy and he checked each one off as they reported ready. In three minutes he turned to Captain Harkins and said:

"The engineers are ready."

The Goliath was ready to test its wings. For a moment it hung, poised just above the ground. Then Captain Harkins nodded again, Andy's whistle shrilled the "lines away" call and the Goliath floated upward into the heavens. For the moment it was the world's largest balloon, drifting upward in the warm rays of the afternoon sun, lifted higher and higher by the buoyancy of its helium gas.

Andy, Bert and Serge were grouped at one of the windows in the control cabin together. The ground simply floated away from them. There was no sense of sudden rising; no undue motion to the great craft.

Fifty, one hundred and then two hundred feet the Goliath climbed into the skies, its powerful motors purring smoothly and ready to take up their task.

Andy cut in the general connection to all of the engine rooms and warned the engineers to stand by for further orders.

When the Goliath was three hundred feet above the field, Captain Harkins turned to Andy and gave the order for slow speed ahead.

"Slow speed ahead," Andy repeated into the transmitter.

The Goliath came to life almost instantly. The great gas bag shook itself as though getting accustomed to its new power and then moved slowly ahead, the ground beneath drifting away in a fascinating panorama.

Captain Harkins, at the controls, moved the wheel which operated the elevators at the tail of the Goliath, and the earth dropped rapidly away from them as they climbed for altitude and circled over the home field. Andy, looking down, could see the members of the ground crew, faces upturned, watching their every move.

The great moment had come and passed. The Goliath had soared aloft and even now was proving the claims of its builders. Captain Harkins ordered half speed ahead and Andy repeated the command to the engine rooms. The speed quickened as the beat of the motors increased but so carefully insulated were the engine rooms that there was no unpleasant or disturbing noise.

The air corps officers appeared elated at the ease with which the Goliath handled and they were outspoken in their praise of the engineers and staff which had constructed the new king of the skies.

For half an hour the Goliath cruised leisurely around the field, now climbing, now dipping lower at the will of the silent man at the controls.

Andy turned his telephone set over to Bert to relay Captain Harkins' commands to the engine rooms and in company with his father, made an inspection of the whole ship.

There had been no shifting of the big gas bags and stress and strain indicators on the transverse rings of duralumin, the real backbone of the dirigible, exceeded their expectations. Engine performance was more than satisfactory and before returning to the control cabin, they mounted one of the stairways to an observation cockpit on the top of the Goliath.

Ahead and behind them stretched the smooth, silvered surface of the Goliath. Far to the east, were the haze enshrouded mountains while below them was the rich, fresh green of the countryside in spring.

Andy stood close to his father for he knew how much the successful flight of the new dirigible meant to the vice president of the National Airways. His father, with Captain Harkins, had dreamed and planned for years for the Goliath, and the culmination of their hopes meant their life careers. Andy, himself, had shouldered no small part of the burden in the studying and engineering necessary for the construction of the huge ship but he felt his own share small in comparison to the manifold burdens which his father had carried. They stood together in the observation cockpit, happy in the knowledge that the Goliath represented a great task well done.

"Son," said Charles High, "I'm mighty proud of all that you've done in the building of the Goliath."

"And I'm mighty proud of you, Dad," said Andy, "for I have some idea of the obstacles you've had to face and the problems you've been called on to solve. The Goliath is certainly an accomplishment for which the world will pay you tribute."

"I'm not looking for tribute or praise," replied his father. "Satisfaction in knowing that the job is done, and done well, is all that I ask. Now I'm looking forward to the day when our plant here at Bellevue and the Goodyear-Zeppelin people at Akron will be busy all the time turning out air cruisers like the Goliath; when the country will be crossed with a network of dirigible lines carrying passengers, express and valuable freight at a high rate of speed and much more safely than airplanes."

"The day is coming and it is not so far in the dim and distant future," said Andy confidently.

A telephone in the observation cage buzzed and Andy answered the call. It was Bert, warning them that Captain Harkins was about to descend.

"We'd better get back to the control cabin," said Andy's father, and they hurried down the ladder, along the main interior runway, and into the control room where Captain Harkins was giving Bert orders to relay to the engine rooms.

With power on, the Goliath nosed down for its first landing. The ground crew was strung out along the field, ready to grasp the lines which would be dropped while the portable mooring mast had been maneuvered into position for the landing.

They were dropping rapidly but smoothly and there was only a slight feeling of downward motion. Captain Harkins checked the forward speed of the Goliath, lines were dropped, and the big ship was back to earth after a flight in which it had lived up to the fondest hopes of its designers and builders.

The nose was pushed up against the mooring mast where the automatic coupling was made and the slow entry into the berth in the hangar started with the mooring mast, on its tractor-truck, waddling along ahead and the Goliath following obediently.

In fifteen minutes the big ship was in its berth and the "orange peel" doors were rolling shut.

Before leaving the gondola, Captain Harkins and Andy's father held a conference with the air corps officers who had made the trip with them and definite plans for the first long trial flight were made. Captain Harkins turned to Andy when the conference was over.

"See that orders are issued for the crew to be aboard ship and ready to depart at three in the morning," he said. "We're going to make a surprise visit to Washington if the weather reports at 2 A. M. are fair."

CHAPTER XIII
Wings of the Storm

Captain Harkins' announcement that the Goliath would make its first long test flight the next morning meant hours of work ahead for Andy but the assistant pilot of the airship threw himself into the task with his usual unfailing energy. He had able assistants in Serge and Bert.

The visit to Washington was to be a complete surprise and every effort was made to keep the news from getting out from Bellevue. If all went well the first intimation the capital would have of the visit of the new sky king would be when the rising sun silvered the nose of the Goliath with its rays.

Andy received detailed reports from each of the engine rooms on the performance during the trip over the field and found them highly satisfactory. Fuel consumption had been less than he had anticipated. Supplies for the flight the next day must be ordered and placed aboard for breakfast and lunch would be served to the army officers and to the members of the crew. Serge volunteered to attend to that task while Bert kept his radio busy getting the latest weather reports. He asked the Washington bureau for a special report at two o'clock the next morning and Washington came back with:

"What's up? Are you chaps going to make a trial flight at that hour of the night?"

Bert refused to give the curious operators at Washington any information but secured the promise that he could have a special meteorological report at the desired hour.

Preparations for the flight were completed by early evening and members of the crew were ordered to bed by nine o'clock. They would be aroused shortly after two if the weather report at that hour was favorable for their plans.

At eight that night the three young friends gathered in Bert's radio shack to talk with Harry, now well out to sea in the Neptune. They picked up Harry's signal on time to the minute and learned that the Neptune had been having a bad time of it.

"I've been sick most of the day," said Harry miserably. "The sea got mighty choppy this morning and we've been tossed all over the inside of this tin fish. The air's bad, too, and it's been so rough we couldn't have eaten much if we had felt like it."

"That's too bad," replied Bert, "but it's just what you get for gallivanting around the world in a cast-iron cigar."

"When is the Goliath going to test its wings?" asked Harry.

"Can't tell you," replied Andy, who had picked up the microphone.

"You mean you won't tell me," said Harry.

"I guess that's it," admitted Andy, "but the first long flight is supposed to be a surprise trip and if I told you where and when we were going to take the air someone with a low wave set might pick it up and the newspapers would spread it all over their front pages."

"I get you," replied Harry. "When shall I come on the air again."

Andy turned to Bert, cutting off the mike temporarily.

"We ought to be over Washington around six o'clock," he said. "How about having Harry tune in then and we'll talk to him while we're circling over the capital?"

"Fine idea," replied Bert enthusiastically. "Make it six o'clock and I'll make a note of it now and put it on my instrument board on the Goliath. If I don't I may get so excited I'll forget to call Harry and he'll be sitting around out there in the ocean wondering what has happened."

Andy cut in the mike again.

"Turn on your juice tomorrow morning at six o'clock, eastern standard time," he told Harry. "I'm going to sign off now. We're rolling out early in the morning and I need a little 'shut-eye'."

Andy, accompanied by Bert and Serge, made a final inspection of the Goliath. Everything was in readiness for the early morning flight. They returned to their rooms at the hotel but sleep was a long time in coming for Andy. He had worked so many long months over the plans and on the actual construction of the Goliath that their realization had seemed, until now, an almost unattainable dream. But now the Goliath was ready to claim its place as the king of all the man-made crafts which cruised the heavens for only that afternoon the great dirigible had tested its wings and found them strong and reliable. On the morrow it would sail away into the eastern sky on its first long trip.

Andy finally fell asleep but in his ears was the steady beat of the Goliath's engines, the sweetest music of all to him.

Bert had left a call at the hotel desk for 1:45 o'clock and he was at his receiving set promptly at two for the special meteorological report from Washington.

The report promised fair weather with a light west wind and an unlimited ceiling.

Bert copied the report in triplicate, placed one copy in his own files for a record and hastened back to the hotel with the other two. He awakened Andy and read the report to the assistant pilot.

"That means we sail at three," said Andy, as he rubbed the sleep from his eyes and hurriedly got into his clothes.

"I'll go wake Dad and Captain Harkins," he added.

"Here's a copy of the report for them," said Bert as he handed Andy the third tissue he had made.

Andy awakened his father and the commander of the Goliath and they agreed that weather conditions were ideal for the flight to Washington.

By two-thirty the hangar was ablaze with light as the members of the crew, their eyes still heavy with sleep, hurried to their posts. Motors were given a final going over, rigging was thoroughly checked, the water ballasts tanks and the water condenser at the top of the big bag were inspected. Finally the Goliath was pronounced ready to go.

At two forty-five the big doors at the end of the hangar started to roll back on their tracks and Andy, from his post in the control room, could hear the roar of engines as the army pilots, assigned to fly with the Goliath on any of its longer trips, warmed up their craft. Four of the army planes under the command of Lieutenant Crummit would accompany the Goliath on the trip to Washington.

The air corps board which was to pass on the performance of the dirigible climbed aboard. Captain Harkins took his place at the main control station and Andy's whistle shrilled for the ground crew to take hold.

The whistle sounded again and the tractor-truck with the portable mooring mast lurched into motion and the Goliath moved slowly ahead. The big ship was walked out into the soft moonlight, which bathed it with its radiance.

Andy gave a general order for the 12 engine rooms to stand by. Then followed the order to start the engines and the night was broken by the subdued roar of the powerful motors.

"All lights out except the riding lights," said Captain Harkins and Andy turned to the bank of switches to carry out the command. Only the shaded lights over the instruments in the control room and those in the engine rooms were left on.

Down the field Andy could see the sputtering stream of fire from the exhausts of the four army planes which were to escort them on the flight to Washington. They would take off as soon as the Goliath was clear of the field.

Reports checked back to Andy from the engine rooms indicated that every motor was functioning perfectly and Andy relayed the report on to Captain Harkins.

Bert, who had kept tuned in on Washington, hurried into the control room, a hastily penciled message in his hand.

Captain Harkins took the message, held it down under one of the shaded lights, and read it aloud so that everyone in the control room could hear.

"Weather from Kentucky east to Atlantic seaboard fair; light west wind; unlimited visibility."

"The weather reports continues favorable," said Captain Harkins. Then, turning to Andy, he said:

"Give the signal for the ground crew to let go."

Andy stepped to the open window. In the moonlight below he could see the line of workmen stretched back into the shadows under the great hulk. His whistle shrilled the release signal. The ground crew let go their hold on the great gas bag and at the same moment the operator of the mooring mast released the automatic coupling.

There was only the slightest tremble as the Goliath started upward. The ground dropped silently away. Below Andy could see the streaks of flame from the exhausts of the fast army planes. A few lights glowed in Bellevue itself but the rest of the country seemed asleep. The

Goliath rose to a level with the hills which enclosed the valley and drifted steadily upward, the beat of its engines muffled by the interior engine room as the powerful motors waited for the command to start driving the dirigible through the air.

"Tell the engine rooms to stand by," said Captain Harkins. A moment later Andy got the command of slow speed ahead and he felt the Goliath gather itself for the trip through the night. The big ship felt steadier with the power on and he leaned from his window to listen to the steady monotone of the muffled exhausts.

Lights of the field drifted out of sight and they slipped over the hills on the start of their surprise visit to Washington. Gradually the speed was stepped up. Forty, fifty, sixty miles an hour they pushed their way through the moonlit sky, soaring through the heavens. The altimeter showed a steady climb and Captain Harkins kept the nose of the Goliath up until they had reached the ten thousand foot level. At that height the muffled sound of the airship's engines could not be heard on the ground and it was doubtful if anyone would see the great silver craft slipping through the sky.

The army planes caught up with them, circled around once or twice, and then climbed five thousand feet above the Goliath, riding the high heavens in unceasing vigilance.

Bert came into the control room again and spoke to Captain Harkins.

"Washington wants to know what's up," said Bert. "What shall I tell them?"

Captain Harkins looked at his watch. It was three-thirty.

"Tell them they'll have a surprise for breakfast," he said, and Bert returned to his radio cubicle to dispatch the message.

The army inspectors were busy going over the Goliath, checking every detail of the airship's operation, rate of climb, maneuverability, speed, engine performance, fuel consumption and the hundred and one specifications which Uncle Sam had decided must be met by the Goliath before it would be acceptable and the remainder of the federal appropriation paid to the National Airways.

With the engines thoroughly warmed to their task. Captain Harkins increased the speed until the Goliath was racing along at an even 100 miles an hour. There was no sense of motion or undue speed; only the ground slipping away beneath in an ever-changing pattern of lights and shadows. Occasionally the streaking lights of a train would be visible or a larger town could cast its reflection upward, but Captain Harkins shifted his course to avoid the larger cities. Some enterprising newspaperman might catch the muffled beat of the engines and take the surprise element out of their visit to the capital.

Andy checked their position on the map and stepped over to Captain Harkins.

"We'll be over Washington about five-thirty if we maintain our present rate of speed," he said.

"That's too early," replied the commander. "Order the engines down to half speed. We can speed up later if we find we're a little behind."

Andy phoned the order to the engine rooms and the Goliath slowed down to a steady fifty miles an hour, with the distance slipping off its silvered sides like magic miles.

The assistant pilot got permission to leave his post and make a tour of inspection. He stopped at Bert's cubby on his way back into the interior.

"Washington is about crazy with curiosity," grinned Bert, who had a headset on, "He knows we've left the field because our signals are stronger but he doesn't believe we're on our way east. Bet he stretches his neck when we arrive."

"A good many thousand people are going to have Stiff necks before the day's over," smiled Andy. "See you later. I'm going to make a swing around this big weiner."

All lights in the main gondola, except those in the control and radio rooms were out, but enough moonlight came through the windows of the promenade deck for Andy to see his way clearly back to the main catwalk in the interior. The catwalk was well lighted and he passed along under the towering gas cells, filled with the precious helium. The stress and strain meters showed that the duralumin framework was reacting even more favorably than they had dared hope to under the test of actual flight.

Andy continued on until he was in the middle of the ship where the great cargo hold was located. It yawned an empty, dimly lighted space. In the fore part were the quarters for the members of the crew and officers and Andy stepped into the tiny cabin he shared with Bert. The night had been raw when he started and he had put on an extra jacket of heavy brown suede but it was not needed now for with their approach to the eastern seaboard the temperature was climbing steadily.

After leaving his cabin, Andy ran up one of the ladders which led to the top of the dirigible and its observation cockpits. He saw the shadow of someone ahead of him and discovered that Serge, who had been making a trip through the interior, could not resist the temptation and had also gone up top.

"You Americans should be very proud of the Goliath," said Serge. "I have never dreamed of anything so complete. It is a Pullman of the air; every comfort thought of and anticipated."

"The thing that pleases me," said Andy, "is that the ship is so far exceeding every specification set for it. The army men haven't said very much but I can tell that they are highly pleased."

They remained up top for ten of fifteen minutes as the new king of the skies slid through its domain. The sky was reddening in the east with the approach of the new day. The mountains were in the west, smeared with the sullen shadows of a night which seemed reluctant to leave. Before them stretched the smoother country of Virginia.

"We're climbing again," said Andy. "Captain Harkins must be going up so high we won't be heard or seen on the ground."

The army planes, faithful guardians through the night, circled far overhead.

"I don't envy those chaps," grinned Serge. "We are moving so slowly they must find it hard to stay anywhere near us. Lieutenant Crummit told me their low cruising speed was 100 miles an hour. Look how they zig-zag back and forth."

"They'll leave us when we get over Washington and drop down on Bolling field to refuel," said Andy. "By the time we get back to Bellevue they'll be pretty much all in. Handling one of those delicate pursuit ships for eight or ten hours is no picnic."

The red disk of the sun popped into view and Andy and Serge left the observation cockpit and returned to the control room. Captain Harkins had hardly moved since leaving Bellevue but now he turned the main controls over to Andy.

"The course is north, northeast," he said. "Hold her as she is and at 12,000 feet."

"North by northeast," replied Andy, "and at 12,000 feet. Yes sir."

The steward had been busy for the last hour and a hot breakfast was served to the army observers and officers of the dirigible in the main dining salon while the crew had its breakfast in the dining room midships.

Bert brought Andy a cup of coffee and a sandwich but the assistant pilot was too interested in the way the Goliath handled to think of asking for relief so he could go back and have the hot cereal, toast and jam that the others enjoyed.

He was master of their dirigible, the king of the skies, the greatest airship ever built by man! Andy's hands firmly grasped the wheels which controlled the elevators and the rudder. The Goliath responded easily and he swung it a point or two off course to see just how it handled.

Captain Harkins returned from breakfast while Andy was bringing the Goliath back on course.

"Experimenting a little to see how the big boy handles?" asked the commander.

"I couldn't resist," replied Andy.

"I know how you feel," smiled Captain Harkins. "I did a little of it myself while we were over the mountains." He turned to Serge.

"Step up here and take control," he told the young Rubanian, whose mission had once been the destruction of the craft in which they now rode in comfort and security.

Serge smiled gratefully as he accepted Captain Harkins' invitation. It had been months since he had stood at the controls of a dirigible. The last time had been early in the winter when he had guided one of the large Blenkkos over Kratz, the capital of Rubania. The day following that trip he had been ordered into the Gerka and then put on the long distance planes, with the result that he was now in the United States, a member of the crew of the Goliath. It all seemed like a vague dream, his long flight across the ocean, his acceptance at Bellevue as a civilian observer from Friedrichshafen and the final discovery of his identity by Andy and the downfall of Alex Reikoff, dictator of Rubania. Within the hour he would soar over Washington, the capital of the United States, and he felt his body glow with the happiness and contentment that was his.

Captain Harkins checked the position of the Goliath and ordered a slight increase in speed. The sun cleared away the morning mists and the entire countryside lay below them, clothed with the green freshness of the spring.

The commander took over the controls and Andy returned to his station at Captain Harkin's right where he was in a position to relay instantly orders to the engine crews.

Andy, watching ahead intently, was the first to catch the white gleam of the Washington monument and a minute later the dome of the capitol was sighted. The Potomac curved lazily below and they soared over Alexandria, Va; In order to reach Washington at six,

Captain Harkins had dipped further into Virginia than he had first intended and approached Washington from the south and east.

The assistant pilot of the Goliath had made many air trips to Washington but he had never viewed the city from that height and he marveled at the beauty of the capital; its great, gleaming white buildings, its broad boulevards and its stately memorials.

It was just six o'clock when Bert hurried out of the radio room.

"Harry just came in on the air," he said. "Can you get off a minute and we'll say good morning to him?"

Serge relieved Andy at the phones and the assistant pilot accompanied Bert back to the radio cubby, where he was handed a headset.

"Harry wants to know what's up?" chuckled Bert.

"All right," grinned Andy. "Cut him in and then listen to him explode."

Bert made the necessary adjustments and Andy heard Harry's familiar voice.

"Hello, hello, hello," said Andy. "This is the dirigible Goliath, now over the city of Washington, in a special broadcast to the Arctic submarine Neptune, en route from Brooklyn, New York, to Plymouth, England, on the first leg of its trip to the North pole where it will be met this summer by the Goliath for an exchange of mail. This is a beautifully clear spring morning with a light west wind. We are paying a surprise visit to the capital after an unannounced departure this morning at three o'clock from the Goliath's home field at Bellevue, Ky."

Andy heard an excited exclamation and then Harry, now far out to sea in the Neptune, started plying him with questions.

"Are you really over Washington now? How is the Goliath behaving? Why didn't you tell a fellow what you were going to do?"

One by one Andy answered them and before he signed off Harry gave three stirring cheers for the Goliath and the success of its first long flight.

"The weather is still bad," he said as he signed off, "and if you don't get me at eight tonight, don't worry. I'm more than a little seasick and I may not feel up to talking with anyone but I'll be on sure tomorrow morning at eight."

Andy met his father on the way back to the control room and found him jubilant.

"The army board is more than enthusiastic about the performance," he told Andy, "and there is no question but what we will get an immediate approval and payment of the balance of the government appropriation."

"I'm mighty glad to know that, Dad," replied Andy, "for I realize how much the success of the Goliath means to you. It will prove the practicability of these big ships for commercial service and mean we can build more of them for National Airways."

When Andy returned to his post in the control room, they were circling over the heart of the city and losing altitude rapidly for Captain Harkins was coming down to give the early morning risers a close view of the world's largest airship.

They swung out over the Potomac and the crew of the night boat, up from Norfolk, Va., which was just steaming into the tidal basin, waved as the Goliath drifted overhead, its speed now cut down to a mere thirty miles an hour. They cruised over the city at a thousand feet.

News of the Goliath's arrival spread rapidly and hundreds of people flocked into the streets to see the big airship.

Captain Harkins headed for the White House and dropped the airship down to seven hundred and fifty feet. Back of the White House a group of men ceased their game of medicine ball to gaze up at the great silver hulk.

Andy nudged Serge and pointed downward.

"There's the president and his 'medicine ball' cabinet," he said.

"What kind of a cabinet is that?" asked Serge.

"It's the group of men with which the president plays medicine ball," explained Andy. "They get together every morning for their exercise. There's usually the president's personal physician, at least one of his private secretaries and several cabinet members and usually a justice of the supreme court."

Officers and crew of the Goliath lined the windows as they passed over the White House and waved at the group below, which returned the greeting enthusiastically.

Captain Harkins dipped the bow of the airship in salute and then threw over the elevator controls and sent the Goliath to a safer altitude. For an hour they cruised over the capital and its environs, now swinging down into Virginia, idling slowly over Arlington and then back over the capital.

Several of the army officers had been in the radio room, getting in touch with their superiors. When they returned they went into a conference with Captain Harkins and Andy's father. The assistant pilot caught snatches of the conversation. He heard Baltimore, New York and Philadelphia mentioned and his heart leaped as Captain Harkins turned to him and handed over the controls.

"Make one more circle over the city," he said, "and then set your course for Baltimore."

"Yes sir," said Andy. "After Baltimore do we start home?"

"Not yet," replied Captain Harkins, his fine eyes twinkling. "The army men are anxious that New York and Philadelphia get a glimpse of the Goliath so we won't be home until night."

They made a final circle of the city and Andy set the course for Baltimore. Serge, at the telephone, relayed the order for the engines to increase their speed to eighty miles and hour and in less than half an hour they were within sight of the city that made the oyster famous.

News that they had headed toward Baltimore had preceded them and the streets were thick with thousands of people craning their necks to see the sky king. They gave Baltimore a half hour view at two thousand feet and by that time the air was full of planes which circled around them. The faithful army ships had rejoined them and had a busy time chasing newspaper planes whose ambitious photographers insisted on getting too close to the Goliath.

The ever-growing procession left Baltimore and headed north for Philadelphia, which was also given a half hour view of them before they proceeded on toward New York.

Captain Harkins took charge again and set the speed so the Goliath would reach the metropolis during the noon hour when the thousands of down town workers would be out to lunch and free to watch the maneuvers of the airship.

Bert stuck his head out of the radio room and called to Andy.

"I've just picked up a message from Washington to Lakehurst," he said. "The Akron and the Los Angeles are being ordered out to join us in a parade over New York."

"I'd almost like to be on the ground to see it," said Andy, "but I guess I'll be contented and stay here."

The sun mounted toward its zenith as New Jersey unfolded below them and the hangars at Lakehurst grew from tiny dots into good-sized mushrooms, outside which two silver ships were starting to take the air. By the time they were over the home of the naval aircraft, the Akron and Los Angeles were at the two thousand foot level and Captain Harkins radiophoned to both ships to decide on the formation. It was agreed that the Los Angeles would lead with the Akron next and the Goliath, the giant of them all, bringing up the rear, a pageant of the progress of aircraft.

The Los Angeles, slimmer and more graceful than the bulkier Akron or the giant Goliath, took the lead and the other two ships fell in behind.

It was a magnificent fleet that paraded over the Jersey flats that spring morning. To the east rolled the sparkling waters of the Atlantic while ahead of them loomed the spires of Greater New York.

The aerial argosy swung out over the bay, dipped in salute as it circled the Statue of Liberty, and then proceeded over the Battery and up the man-made canyon that is known the world over as Broadway.

Whistles of tugs and ferryboats blended in a concerted shriek of welcome and the streets below were thronged with humanity. Traffic in down town New York was at a standstill, tied up so hopelessly that it took hours to get it moving again.

They passed the mooring mast atop the Empire State at fifty miles an hour and then dipped slightly to the west to look down on Times Square. Central park displayed its greenery ahead of them and in another minute they were over Riverside drive and the Hudson.

Captain Harkins shifted the course and they turned and cut across Manhattan to give Brooklyn a view of the Goliath. For an hour and a half the three dirigibles zigzagged back and forth over the metropolitan area. At one-thirty the command was given to start for home and with the final scream of whistles in their ears, the crew of the

Goliath watched the mighty buildings of Manhattan disappear behind them.

Lunch was served while they were on the return to Lakehurst, where the Los Angeles and the Akron left them and they proceeded on toward Bellevue accompanied only by the four army planes.

Captain Harkins set a bee-line course that took them over New Jersey, west of Philadelphia, and across the heart of the mountains to their sheltered valley home in Kentucky.

Bert had obtained a mid-afternoon weather forecast from Washington, which he handed to Andy. The prediction was none too favorable. A storm had swept down off the Great Lakes and was now over Ohio. If it continued its present rate and course it would bisect the path of the Goliath. Andy passed the forecast on to Captain Harkins, whose lips tightened into a firm, straight line.

"Looks like we'll be in for some nasty weather before we get home," observed the commander of the Goliath. "Keep in touch with Washington, Bert, and advise me at once of any changes in the weather report."

Captain Harkins ordered the speed stepped up until they were doing an even ninety an hour. In calm weather they would have been averaging a hundred but a westerly wind cut them down ten miles an hour.

Clouds rolled out of the west and the sun was obscured by the drifting banks of gray.

Bert came back to the control room to say that weather reports now indicated spotty weather all of the way home with local showers and thunderstorms.

They ran under a bank of rain clouds and the Goliath got its first taste of dirty weather, but it rode through the shower without difficulty, the rain shooting off its metalized sides in steady sheets.

Dusk found them two hundred miles from Bellevue with storms all around them. Lightning was flashing steadily in the northwest and the sky was full of wind squalls with the clouds rolling and twisting in an ominous manner.

"Just the kind of a night for a tornado," Andy heard his father tell Captain Harkins in a low voice. The Commander of the Goliath, his face lined with worry, nodded.

The storm was thickening. It would break at any minute. They had stuck to their course as long as they dared before Captain Harkins gave the orders to run before the storm. The Goliath heeled sharply as a vicious gust of wind caught it broadside while it was circling. Then they were running into the southeast with the storm behind them.

Electrical interference was so heavy that it was impossible for Bert to communicate with the Washington weather bureau and learn the conditions they were running into. They simply had to take the course of the least resistance and hope that they could escape the fury of the elements.

For half an hour the Goliath sped through the heavy night. Rain beat against its silvered sides and flashes of lightning cast their glare over the boiling clouds. If the big airship returned to Bellevue without mishap it would certainly have won its laurels on its maiden flight.

The weather was getting thicker and Captain Harkins ordered Andy and Serge into the observation cockpits on top of the big bag.

"Keep in constant touch with me," he ordered. "If you see a break in the storm let me know and we'll try and run through it."

From their lonely posts atop the dirigible Andy and Serge, clad in oilskins, braced themselves against the heat of the rain and the rush of the wind. With headsets on their ears and transmitters slung across their chests, they kept in touch with the main control room. All around them was a sea of churning clouds, rolling thunder, bolts of glittering blue and through it all the steady beat of the powerful engines as they drove the Goliath on through the night.

They were at the seven thousand foot level and Captain Harkins warned them he was going to attempt to get above the storm. The nose shot skyward and they pushed their way up through the clouds. Eight, nine and ten thousand feet dropped away, but even at that level the storm raged. There was no escape. Flickers of static played along the runway atop the Goliath and Andy was grateful that the gas cells were filled with the non-explosive helium.

At ten thousand feet the Goliath was making the fight for its life. Grim-faced engineers watched over their engines while in the control room Captain Harkins and Andy's father stood side by side as they guided the great airship through the storm. The army officers, grouped close behind, watched every move for their lives hung in the balance that fateful night. Would the storm rip the Goliath asunder and drop it, a broken, lifeless thing, like it had the Shenandoah? Would their fate be the same? Those questions were in the mind of every man.

The storm increased in violence and Andy, atop the dirigible, felt the frame trembling under the terrific blows from the wind. He looked about desperately for some break in the clouds that would let them through to safety. The Goliath was making a brave battle but it was only a question of how long it could stand such a battering.

Bert, down in the control room, was on the other end of the phone, and the news he gave Andy was none too encouraging. No. 5 engine had cut out. The crew reported a burned out bearing, which meant that the engine was disabled for the remainder of the trip. Ten minutes later No. 9 on the opposite side developed trouble and had to be shut down. They were cruising with 10 motors running, ample power for any average storm but this spring disturbance of the weather was anything but usual.

An occasional brilliant glare of lightning would reveal Serge at his observation post further back along the top and Andy wondered how the young Rubanian was faring. If they could only locate a break in the clouds. Andy's eyes swept the darkness again but it was to no avail.

The Goliath heeled savagely and he clung to the edge of the cockpit. They were knifing off to the right. The speed of the motors had increased. Could the men in the control room have sighted a break or had Serge's eyes been keener than his own?

The Goliath was running for its life, pulsating to the throbbing power of the engines. They must be doing well over a hundred, thought Andy.

The clouds ahead thinned; the rain lessened, the force of the wind abated and in ten more minutes they were out of the main storm, sailing through a light spring shower. Andy dropped down on a seat in the observation cockpit. He was exhausted for he had fought every step with the

Goliath and now that safety was at hand he felt a great wave of fatigue sweep over him.

After a five minute rest he descended into the heart of the dirigible and then made his way forward to the control room. Captain Harkins was still at the controls but the lines of his face had softened.

"We're through the worst of it," he told Andy. "We'll loaf along here until the weather north and west of us clears enough so we can get back to Bellevue. You take charge while I go back for a bite to eat. I'm pretty much all in."

All Andy knew was that they were somewhere over the western part of the Carolinas, and he let the Goliath ease through the night at a bare thirty-five miles an hour. The rain ceased and the moon was struggling to break through the clouds.

Bert had managed to get in touch with Washington and allayed the fears of officials at the capital. He also learned that the four army planes which had accompanied the Goliath had landed safely in West Virginia. This was good news to Andy, who in his concern over the safety of the Goliath had forgotten the army flyers.

Serge came down from his observation post and Captain Harkins praised him highly.

"It was Serge," he told Andy, "who spotted the break in the storm. If it hadn't been for his keen eyes one guess is as good as another as to where we would be now."

By ten o'clock the storms had drifted away and they were free to start the return to Bellevue. The trouble on No. 9 motor had been repaired and with only No. 5 out, they sped toward home.

The lights of Bellevue came into view at eleven-fifteen and ten minutes later the Goliath drifted down to stick its squat nose into the automatic coupling on the portable mooring mast. Eager hands steadied the great ship as it was towed into the hangar and lodged securely in its berth.

Before leaving the hangar, a thorough inspection was made to ascertain if any sections had undergone damage during the storm. The outer fabric was in perfect condition and outside of the failure of No. 5 motor, the Goliath had won its laurels in its first long flight.

CHAPTER XIV
Flood Relief

News of the Goliath's victorious battle against the most severe storm of the spring was spread on the front page of every newspaper in the country the next day and special writers and correspondents for the big press associations besieged the military patrol at Bellevue. Venturesome photographers even attempted to fly over the plant and snap pictures of the hangar but the army planes soon put an end to that stunt.

The insistence of the reporters compelled the attention of Andy's father and Captain Harkins, and they called Andy into their conference. He advised that reporters be escorted through the hangar and taken on a thorough trip over the dirigible.

"We want the public to have faith in the Goliath," counseled Andy, "and the reporters must have the facts if they are to write intelligently."

"I believe you're right," agreed his father and Captain Harkins added a word of approval.

Andy and Bert were designated as the tour conductors and they met the reporters at the hotel. Nine men and two women were in the group they escorted to the plant.

Andy was amused by their exclamations of wonder at the size of the Goliath and he was pleased at their open praise of the beauty of the great ship. The inspection tour required two hours that afternoon for they went into every part of the dirigible, even up to the observation cockpits on top and several of the more daring reporters walking along the upper catwalk.

When they returned to the main cabin, they found that Captain Harkins had ordered the steward to serve tea. It was late afternoon by the time the reporters departed, but they left highly elated over their expedition and promised that glowing stories of the Goliath would appear in their papers and on the press association wires.

When they had gone, Andy and Bert sat down on the steps of the hotel. The tension of fighting with the Goliath through the storm of the night before had carried them along but now they relaxed and an enveloping cloak of fatigue settled over them.

"I'm so tired I can hardly wiggle," groaned Bert.

"I'm just about that bad," agreed Andy. "Believe me, I'll go to bed early tonight."

"Wonder what's happened to Harry and the Neptune?" said Bert. "I managed to roll out this morning in time to tune in at eight o'clock but I didn't get even a peep out of him."

"I must have been sound asleep when you got up," said Andy, "for I didn't hear a thing."

"I came back to bed after failing to get in touch with Harry," replied Bert. "I'll try again tonight at eight. Hope I have better luck. I wouldn't trust one of those tin fish as far as I could throw my hat. They don't look safe to me."

"I expect a sailor feels the same way about an airship," said Andy. "It all depends on what you're used to."

After dinner that night Andy's father announced that special tests would be made the next week, including the attaching of a plane to the Goliath while in flight. This had been successfully accomplished by the Akron and they expected no difficulty. The special rigging was already at

Bellevue and it would be only the matter of a few days to complete the installation. The Goliath differed from the Akron in one capacity. Where the Akron could carry a single plane slung underneath in a special carriage, the Goliath had a special hold midships where the planes could be raised and stored. It could accommodate four fast pursuit ships, launching them as it sped through the air at one hundred miles an hour. It was from this viewpoint that the Goliath held unusual value to the army officers.

Shortly before eight o'clock Andy and Bert went to the radio room, where Bert tuned up his receiver for a talk with Harry, now far out to sea in the Neptune.

He turned on the power at eight o'clock and waited patiently for a signal from the submarine. When it failed to come he tried calling Harry but even then failed to get a reply.

Bert worked for an hour hoping that he could get some answer from the Neptune but at nine o'clock was forced to admit defeat.

"I'm getting worried," confessed Bert. "It was too stormy to make contact last night so it's been nearly 36 hours since we've heard from Harry and anything can happen out there in mid-ocean."

"Don't let your imagination run away with you," counseled Andy, who admitted to himself that he was afraid some accident had befallen the Neptune. "They've probably run into a streak of bad weather and may have submerged to try and ride it out."

"I'll try again the first thing in the morning," said Bert. "We've just got to hear from Harry," he added desperately.

In spite of their fatigue, Andy and Bert passed a restless night and they were up with the first sign of the dawn. Without waiting for breakfast they hurried to the radio room where Bert tuned in on the wave length used for communication between the station at Bellevue and the Neptune.

"Someone's on the air," he said quickly. "I can hear the hum of his transmitter; sounds like Harry's set."

"Hello, Neptune," said Bert. "This is the station at Bellevue, Ky., calling for the submarine Neptune, now en route to Plymouth, England. Hello, Neptune, hello!"

Andy bent close to the loud speaker, waiting eagerly for the ether waves to bring a reply to Bert's call.

It failed to come and Bert repeated his call. Still there was no answer and the call went out a third and then a fourth time.

"I can't understand his failure to reply," said Bert. "His set is running."

"Try it once more," urged Andy. "Maybe we'll have better luck."

Bert repeated his call and then gazed at Andy incredulously as Harry's familiar voice replied almost immediately.

"You must be a prophet," Bert told Andy. "Where in the dickens have you been for the last two days?" he asked Harry. "We've been scared stiff for fear your tin fish might have sunk."

"No such luck," replied Harry. "I've been so seasick I couldn't even sit up. This is my first message since I last talked with you two days ago."

"Been running into rough weather?" asked Andy.

"I never dreamed the ocean could be so nasty," replied Harry in a hollow voice. "We've been tossed around like a cork and half the crew has been under the weather. This morning is the first time in 48 hours we could cruise on the surface with any degree of comfort."

"Don't blame us for your predicament," said Bert unfeelingly. "I warned you to keep out of the submarine. But, no, you knew best."

"Listen," replied Harry. "I couldn't let you go to the North Pole and slip one over on me so when I heard the Neptune was going to make the trip I signed up. You fellows wait until old man weather gets a real good shot at you and you won't think it is quite so funny."

"We've had our turn," said Andy, and he told Harry in detail of the events which had occurred on their return from New York and of their strenuous battle against the elements.

"Looks to me like the Goliath and the Neptune proved their ability at about the same time," said Harry. "After the last two days in the Neptune, I've got every confidence in it."

"I called you for fifteen minutes before you answered," said Bert. "Your transmitter was on the air but I couldn't get any reply."

"The answer is simple," replied Harry. "I wasn't here. As I said before, I've been feeling pretty rocky. Well, I came up to the radio room and turned on the set, intending to call you. Then I got shaky again and had to go back and lie down. Guess I forgot to turn off the set and it kept buzzing away."

"How much longer will it take you to reach Plymouth?" asked Andy.

"With the delay we've encountered on account of the storm, it will take nearly another week," replied Harry, "and here's hoping that we'll have fair weather from now on."

They signed off a few minutes later after agreeing to talk again that night at eight o'clock.

The remainder of that day and the rest of the week was devoted to the installation of the special landing apparatus which would snare a plane out of mid-air and haul it safely into the inner hold of the Goliath.

Andy and Bert talked with Harry every day and learned that the Neptune, aided by favorable weather, was making good progress. The sea had steadied down and Harry had found his sea legs and his appetite had returned.

"Which means," laughed Bert, "that the cook aboard that sub is going to have a man-sized job keeping Harry filled with food."

Air corps officers from various posts flew in to inspect the Goliath while the members of the official board which had accompanied the airship on its flight to New York remained at hand for further tests. It was Tuesday of the following week before the installation of the special gear had been completed and the Goliath pronounced ready for further tests.

The pursuit ship of Lieutenant Crummit was also fitted with special rigging and when this was completed they were ready for another trial.

Tuesday was an ideal spring day with plenty of sunshine and only a slight breeze from the south. The Goliath was walked out of its hangar and, with Captain Harkins at the controls and Andy at his side, made its third trip aloft.

When they were well under way, Andy went back midships to supervise the contact with the pursuit plane.

Lieutenant Crummit buzzed nervously about the Goliath in his fast single-seater. The airship gradually stepped up its speed until it was doing a hundred miles an hour, going fast enough for the contact to be made.

Back in the cavernous hold of the Goliath a tense crew was waiting to leap to its task. Andy's father came back to watch the operation.

A great arm hung beneath the dirigible and from this arm extended a V-shaped coupler into which the coupler on the plane would fit. Synchronization of speed was the main thing upon which success depended and it was up to Lieutenant Crummit to creep up under the Goliath at just a trifle more than a hundred miles an hour.

From the observation windows in the keel Andy watched the approach of the pursuit plane. Lieutenant Crummit was coming in as slowly as he dared, maneuvering carefully in an attempt to make the coupling on the first contact.

The triangular coupling mounted on the upper wing of the army plane slipped into the "V" of the arm below the Goliath. There was a slight jolt at the shock of contact and Lieutenant Crummit, assured that the coupling was fast, cut the switches on his motor and looked up expectantly.

Andy threw over the switch on the main control. The large trap door at the bottom of the Goliath rolled back. Simultaneously the arm which held the army plane fast in its grip moved upward rapidly, bringing the pursuit ship with it. In another thirty seconds the army fighter was deposited safely in the hold, the trap door was back in place and the powerful crane, or arm, which had caught and lifted the plane, was back in position.

Lieutenant Crummit leaped from the cockpit and ran toward Andy.

"That's the greatest aerial stunt I've ever seen," he said. "Why, it's as simple as falling off a log. I couldn't miss that big 'V' and the next thing I knew the plane was being whirled upward."

Army officers who had watched the operation from the control room came back to interview the lieutenant and get his report. It was decided to repeat the maneuver, only this time the plane would be set into flight from the Goliath.

The large crane was lifted back into the hold and made fast to the plane. When Lieutenant Crummit signalled he was ready, Andy opened the trap door and dropped the plane through. The army flyer switched on his inertia starter, the warm motor caught the first time over and the propeller went into its dazzling whirl.

Lieutenant Crummit threw up his left arm as a signal for the release and the big crane relinquished its grip on the pursuit ship. The army plane dropped down and away from the Goliath, then climbed and raced wildly around the mother ship. The Goliath had passed another one of its exacting tests successfully and Andy returned to the main control room and relieved Serge, who had taken his place during his absence in the hold.

Instead of heading back for Bellevue, the Goliath swung north and Andy looked inquiringly at his father, who had just returned from a conference with the army men.

"We're going to give Cincinnati a treat," said the vice president of the National Airways. "We can make the trip up there and be back home before dark."

With Lieutenant Crummit's plane and another army craft as escorts, the Goliath roared northward at a hundred miles an hour, knifing its silver hull through the lazy, fleecy clouds.

The Ohio river, heavy-burdened with a spring flood, rolled ahead of them and just beyond was the haze which hung over Cincinnati. It was a surprise visit but the townspeople were not long in hurrying into the streets to glimpse the king of the air. They wheeled and turned over Cincinnati for a half hour before heading back for Bellevue.

Bert, who had left his radio room, leaned out a window and looked down at the swollen Ohio.

"There's plenty of water rolling down to the Gulf," he told Andy, "and from all reports the Ohio isn't the only river on a rampage. Almost every large tributary of the Mississippi is at flood stage, which means plenty of trouble for people living down in the lower river country. It will take several days for the flood waters to get there, but when they do the country is going to forget about the Goliath and think about the flood."

"You're a cheerful sort of a soul," smiled Andy.

"Just mark my words," insisted Bert. "I predict a big flood on the lower portions of the Mississippi."

They returned to Bellevue as twilight was draping its mantle of soft purple over the valley and it was dark, by the time the Goliath was in its berth.

There were minor adjustments and changes to be made on the Goliath and the next three days were busy ones for the officers and members of the crew.

Bert's prediction was coming true, if the stories appearing in the papers were not exaggerating the situation. From Memphis down the Mississippi was on a rampage, crashing through the man-made barriers that had been erected to keep it in its channel and spreading death and destruction over large areas of fertile land.

The Friday morning paper, which reached Bellevue by bus shortly after noon, emphasized the need for relief measures, stressing that refugees were without proper clothes or food. The national Red Cross had stepped in and was making every effort to relieve the situation but it was impossible to reach some of the more isolated regions and women and children were believed to be in want.

"What they need is a dirigible," said Andy. "Why, we could load the Goliath with tons of food and clothing, cruise over that area at a low altitude, and drop supplies for hundreds of refugees."

"Why don't you suggest it to your father?" said Bert.

"I'll do it right now," said Andy, and he started toward the hotel.

Charles High heard his son's story without comment and when Andy was through, spoke with his characteristic decision.

"I'll put through a call to the national Red Cross office in Washington," he said, "and if the need is as serious as you feel, we'll start before dawn."

The national headquarters of the Red Cross confirmed the emergency and welcomed the offer of the National Airways to send the Goliath into the flood region. Arrangements were made to bring in supplies on a special train from Cincinnati and the loading of the Goliath was set for shortly after midnight.

The special train arrived an hour late and the crew of the airship worked with feverish haste to transfer the clothes and food from the express cars to the Goliath. The task was completed at four o'clock and with the first tints of dawn in the sky, the Goliath was taken out of its hangar and started on its errand of mercy.

Captain Harkins held the big ship at a steady eighty miles an hour and by mid-forenoon they were well below Memphis and swinging over the flood area. The Mississippi had turned its valley into an immense brown lake. The waters had swilled through towns, inundating streets and sweeping houses from their foundations.

Many of the towns had been deserted while others, on higher ground, were completely cut off by the flood. It was to the latter that the Goliath was directed.

Bert kept in touch with the latest radio reports on the conditions and the Goliath swung from one village to another. Andy, back in the hold, superintended the dropping of food and clothes. The food was put into bundles of clothes and then dropped overboard, the Goliath descending until it was a bare fifty feet above the towns to which it brought relief. With motors shut off, it was possible for Andy to carry on a conversation with the marooned people and ascertain their needs. Serge was with Andy and they directed the crew in the relief work.

Through the morning and afternoon they worked and their supply of food and clothing dwindled at a surprising rate. Two more towns to serve and they would be through. They dropped food and clothing to the first one and hurried on to supply the second. After that they would start for home.

Lieutenant Crummit and another army flyer had stuck with them all day long, leaving only when it was necessary to fly to some city and replenish their fuel supply, but one of the army pursuit ships had always been on duty.

A scene of complete desolation greeted them as they neared the last town to which they were bringing assistance. Flood waters were pouring through every street and the inhabitants who had not escaped were huddled on house tops. More than fifty men, women and children were congregated on the flat roof of a garage, the largest building in the town. Out of the northwest a chill wind was presaging a raw, bitter night and Andy shivered as he thought of the suffering which the little band on the rooftop would undergo before rescuers could reach them by boat.

"Why don't we drop down and take them aboard?" suggested Bert. "With much more exposure some of those people will have pneumonia."

"It might be possible," agreed Andy. "We'll see Captain Harkins."

They presented their suggestion to the commander of the Goliath, and, after a careful survey, Captain Harkins agreed. Orders were given for the descent of the Goliath and Andy went back midships to supervise the dropping of a flexible steel ladder. The Goliath could not land directly on the roof, but would hover just above it. The refugees would have to climb the ladder to safety.

With a megaphone in his hands, Andy directed the rescue work. The Goliath, its motors turning over just enough to hold it above the roof, hung almost motionless. The excited townspeople grasped the ladder, which four men held fast to the rooftop. The ladder was none too steady but the refugees, preferring the climb to the airship to another night on the rooftop, bravely made their way aloft. Women came up alone with the boys and girls following them. Babes in arms were carried up by the men. In fifteen minutes the transfer had been completed, the ladder was drawn up, the command given to proceed and the refugees hurried forward into the main cabin where it was warm and where the stewards had prepared a hot meal.

It was a grateful group that came into the control room later to express their thanks to Captain Harkins, but the commander referred them to Andy, saying:

"You can thank Andy High, assistant pilot, for he was the one who directed the rescue."

They made the run back to Memphis without difficulty but it was well after dark when they soared over the city. Bert had radioed the story of the rescue and the news that they would stop at Memphis and leave the refugees. The airport was aglow with lights and when the Goliath nosed down for an easy landing, police were taxed to the utmost to keep back the cheering throng.

Flashlights boomed as newspaper photographers snapped the refugees as they disembarked. The Red Cross was on hand to care for the unfortunate townspeople and after ascertaining that the weather was fair, the Goliath continued its homeward journey.

The next month was a succession of busy days with further tests for the giant airship. Reports from Harry indicated the daily progress of the Neptune toward its goal in the Arctic, first to Plymouth, England, on to Bergen, Norway, then toward the Arctic with the last stop at King's Bay, Spitzbergen.

Preparations at Bellevue were now centering on the flight to the Arctic. Special oils for the motors were arriving as well as equipment and clothing for the officers and crew. Insulation of the engine rooms and the gondola was increased to stand the colder temperatures of the northland. The tentative date for the start of the flight was set for July 10th and the month of June rolled away as though on magic wheels.

Harry radioed from King's Bay that the Neptune was about ready to start the final dash to the pole. On the 20th of June he reported that they were nosing out of the bay, running on the surface. A few hours later came the news that the Coast of Spitzbergen was disappearing over the horizon and that the Neptune was headed north into the land of eternal ice and snow.

The exchange of mail by the Goliath and Neptune had attracted the attention of stamp collectors in all parts of the world and extra mail clerks were brought to Bellevue to handle the hundreds of letters which had been sent there for mailing aboard the Goliath, which would transfer the pouches when it met the Neptune at the North Pole. The amount of mail had been limited to five tons, a total which was reached long before the date for closing the pouches was reached. A special cancellation stamp had been devised to show that the letters had been sent by the Goliath.

With the Neptune definitely slipping through the broken ice of the Arctic, the importance of Bert's task of keeping in touch with the Neptune increased and he almost lived in the radio room of the Goliath.

The days marched by in a steady procession. Daily reports from Harry indicated that ice conditions were most favorable and that the Neptune was finding much clear water. Occasionally it was necessary to dive under some particularly stubborn ice field but this had not happened often.

Then things changed; high winds prevailed in the northland; progress was retarded; ice jammed in front of the Neptune; static set up a wall of interference that was almost impossible to break through; messages from Harry were few and far between, and lines of worry deepened as Bert and Andy waited anxiously in the radio room.

On the 28th of June a wave of static turned back every query sent into the Arctic. On the 29th the same conditions prevailed. When the static cleared on the 30th of June, Bert called in vain for the Neptune but there was no answer.

CHAPTER XV
The Northern Seas

After a rough crossing of the Atlantic from New York to Plymouth, England, where the Neptune had put in to replenish its supply of fuel, the cruise of the polar submarine had been much smoother and Harry had really enjoyed his trip. The daily talks by radiophone with Bert, Serge and Andy were the high spots of the day for he missed the pleasure of their companionship.

His first days aboard the Neptune had been miserable with the weather rough and his stomach turning flip-flops every time he tried to eat. But after leaving Plymouth and heading north for Bergen he had found the sub and its tricks to his liking. Bob Smith, first officer of the Neptune, was not much older than Harry. Bob was a navy man, loaned to Gilbert Mathews especially for the Polar cruise, and he was thoroughly at home in the underwater craft.

From Bergen to King's Bay, Spitzbergen, was a lonely voyage for there are few ships in the Arctic. An occasional gull wheeling overhead, stray bergs drifting by, and the eternal blue of the cold North Atlantic was all they saw day after day. Harry kept the radio humming with the press messages which the explorer sent back to his syndicate in New York. One method Mathews had used in spreading out the cost of the trip was the sale of exclusive stories of what went on aboard the Neptune to a newspaper syndicate. Morning and afternoon stories were required and Harry, who was adept at writing a readable story, was often pressed into service to write the daily dispatch.

Weather favored them all the way to King's Bay, where they were to make their final stop for supplies, which had been sent on ahead by steamers.

Harry deserted his post and went up on deck when Bob called down to inform him that they were slipping into King's Bay, scene of the start of many a famous Arctic flight. It was from here that Byrd and Floyd Bennett had made their dash to the North pole, to be followed a few days later by Nobile and Ellsworth in the Italian dirigible Norge. It was here that Wilkins and Eielson had landed after their long flight from Alaska across the barrens of the Arctic and it was from here that the ill-fated Norge had made a second expedition into the Arctic.

By the time the sleek, black submarine had nosed its way up to the large coal dock, the entire population of King's Bay was down to greet it. The crew and officers welcomed the opportunity to leave the Neptune and stretch their legs on land, but preparations for the trip into the Arctic were pushed with all possible haste. The weather was too favorable for any unnecessary delay and the crew worked steadily at the task of refilling fuel tanks and taking on fresh stores of food.

On the morning of the 20th of June they cast their lines off the coal dock, the big Diesels turned over smoothly, and the Neptune backed away and turned its nose toward the open bay.

As many of the crew of 31 as could crowd onto the deck watched the changing scene, and listened to the wishes for good fortune shouted by the townspeople on the dock. There was a fresh breeze in the outer bay and they were forced below by the crisp wind which sent waves slapping over the deck in steady succession.

They were in the land of the midnight sun where in summer there is no night, only a dusk as the sun dips to the horizon. At dusk the mainland of Spitzbergen was to the rear and they were slipping past Amsterdam island, which lay to their right. Ahead of them was the uncharted mystery of the Arctic ocean.

Harry was surprised at the comparative mildness of the Arctic summer but the temperature of the Arctic sea was not such that a fall overboard was inviting and as a result the outer hull of the craft was ice-cold. Special electrical heating devices had been installed in the living quarters and the control room so it was fairly comfortable inside the sub.

As they pushed northward, Gilbert Mathews and the two scientists with him kept busy in the forward torpedo room where they made soundings of the ocean depth and drew off samples from the bottom to determine the nature of the floor of the Arctic. Because of the scientific investigations, the Neptune made slow progress and it was the fourth day out before they encountered much pack ice.

Conditions were favorable for the progress of the Neptune, for the ice fields were open with wide leads between them. Occasionally a small berg scraped the side of the submarine and on the fifth day, when they encountered a solid mass of ice, the diving order was given and the Neptune, its special electrical feelers projecting ahead, slipped under the wall of ice and into the open water on the other side. Such an operation was under the direct charge of Bob Smith, who demonstrated his ability in that one brief maneuver.

The weather remained fair and on the 26th and 27th, the Neptune increased its speed for the ice was fairly open. They were following almost the same route taken by Byrd and Bennett in their successful dash by air to the North Pole. On the twenty-eighth the sky closed in on them. A cold Arctic fog obscured the sun and a wall of static shut them off from communication with the outside world. They were now well into the unknown regions of the Arctic, further north than any vessel had previously penetrated, in the region which had been seen by man only from the air.

On the night of the twenty-eighth a bitter wind whipped down out of the northwest and the leads commenced to close under the pressure of the drifting ice.

The Neptune scuttled from one open area to another seeking safety but the gravity of the situation increased every minute. With the ice pack closing in, it was possible that the submarine might be caught between the ice and crushed like an egg shell for despite its sturdy construction it could not withstand the enormous pressure which the ice would exert.

Bob was glued to the controls while Gilbert Mathews searched madly for an opening through which the Neptune might slip to safety. There was none and reluctantly the order was given to submerge.

They would be safe down below for the time being but they would be unable to tell in what direction safety lay. They would have to feel their way almost blindly under the ice, hoping that they would eventually find an opening where they could rise to the surface.

Bob sent the Neptune down five fathoms and they slipped under the ice pack.

Hour after hour passed as the Neptune crept under the great mass of ice. At times it was necessary to go down to 10 and 12 fathoms but for the most part they were only five or six fathoms under the ice. The Neptune was a good underwater boat, steady and smooth-riding and the crew experienced little discomfort. There was plenty of air for 40 hours under the ice and they felt no alarm, when, at the end of twenty hours, they had failed to find an opening.

They stopped and made a test with the ice drill which had been especially designed and installed for just such an emergency but the device jammed tight before they could get it working and that avenue of escape was cut off.

When another ten hours had elapsed and they were still groping blindly under the ice. Bob expressed his private opinion that they were in a tight situation. Harry agreed as he stood beside the first officer in the control room. Another three hours slipped away and the air was heavy. Harry's head felt light and the blood raced through his veins. Unless they found an opening soon it would be curtains for the Neptune and its crew. Gilbert Mathews relieved Bob at the main controls and the first officer walked back to the radio cubby with Harry.

"If we don't get out of this," he said, "no one will ever know what happened to us. They'll have plenty of guesses and some of them will be right, but they'll never really know. I wish you could get a message through."

"So do I," said Harry, "but that won't be possible until we emerge."

"I'm all in," confessed Bob, "and I don't suppose worrying will help us any. Wake me up in half an hour," he added as he slumped down in the one comfortable canvas chair in the room.

Harry returned to the control room where a white-faced, worried crew stuck grimly to their stations.

The air was bad; lights dim. They were barely creeping forward. Several of the men dropped at their posts and were carried away by more fortunate companions. Others took their places. The chief engineer, a quiet Yankee, came in to tell the explorer that the power was going. The batteries wouldn't last more than another hour.

There was nothing Harry could do in the control room and he returned to his own quarters. Bob was sound asleep in the chair. One dim light glowed over the now useless radio set. Harry sat down and picked up a message blank. He'd write a note to Andy and Bert. Someone might find the hulk of the submarine some day; a freak of the Arctic might cast it where it would again be viewed by man.

Harry had just started the note when he was startled by a sudden bumping and scraping. The Neptune tilted sharply. Were they headed for the bottom; crushed under the ice pack? The thought shot through Harry's mind as he roused Bob.

There were cries from the control room. They were going up. They had found an opening in the ice pack.

Three minutes later the main hatch was thrown open and a wave of cool, fresh air swept down into the dank, stinking interior of the submarine.

They were in a small lead between the sheer walls of the ice pack. The Neptune had nosed into it blindly at a time when officers and crews had despaired of their own lives.

As soon as the batteries had been charged sufficiently, Harry tried to send out a call but the wall of static still engulfed the Arctic and his efforts were futile.

"I don't think I got out more than a hundred miles," he told Bob, "and there isn't one chance in a thousand that anyone heard us."

The Neptune remained securely in the sheltered lead all day on the 30th, crew and officers resting after the strenuous ordeal they had been through. Above them and over the ice pack a high wind raged and toward the close of day there were ominous crackings and rumblings in the ice.

With the exception of one man left in the conning tower, the crew of the Neptune was sound asleep at midnight. Two hours later they were awakened by the alarmed cries of the watch. An eerie rumbling and groaning filled the night. When they tumbled out on deck a terrifying sight greeted them. The walls of the ice pack were closing in. They were trapped in the lead!

The rapid movement of the ice was astounding. Orders cracked from the lips of Gilbert Mathews and Bob Smith. The crew tumbled back into the submarine. The main hatch was slammed and battened down. A crash dive was in order. They were going under the ice again.

Harry dreaded the thought. The last time their margin of safety had been slim; too slim. This time they might not come up.

The tension inside the Neptune was terrific as Bob gave the orders for the dive. Valves were opened wide; water roared into the diving tanks. The Neptune settled swiftly. The conning tower was almost under when there was a terrific bump. Their downward motion stopped. The water continued to rush into the diving tanks but the depth indicated remained motionless.

"We're caught on an ice shelf," cried the explorer.

"Blow the tanks and we'll get back to the surface," commanded Bob. "We won't have a chance if we're caught by the ice under water."

Compressed air whistled into the diving tanks and the needle of the depth gauge quivered and moved upward. With a rush they were back on the surface.

The walls of the ice had moved closer. There was the steady thunder of the pack as the pressure increased and miles of ice, driven by the biting gale, moved forward, crushing all before it.

Under Gilbert Mathews' direction, members of the crew made hasty soundings. To their dismay it was found that the tremendous pressure of the advancing ice had driven a shelf of it under them. There wasn't a single hole large enough to allow them to dive through to the comparative safety of the depths.

In the next seconds a tremendous decision must be made: Should they stay with the Neptune or abandon the submarine and attempt to escape over the ice?

The walls of ice were moving forward relentlessly, closing the gap foot by foot.

Gilbert Mathews, white-faced, grim, spoke.

"Get out the emergency equipment," he said. "We'll abandon the Neptune."

For the next ten minutes the crew worked desperately. Food, tents, snowshoes, medical supplies, and the portable radio and stoves were rushed up from below. The Neptune was nosed over against the nearest wall of ice and the supplies tossed on the pack. Others of the crew, hurrying over the treacherous ice, carried the supplies back to a place of safety for the tremendous pressure which would be exerted when the walls of ice met might cause an explosion.

Harry took a final look at his beloved set before abandoning the Neptune. He tried one more desperate call but the static strangled his cry for help. They were alone in the desolate Arctic.

The Neptune abandoned to its fate, the crew retired from the edge of the ice pack. From a distance of half a mile they watched the walls of ice come together. Gilbert Mathews turned away when the first of the rumbling explosions shattered the air. Ice rose in great pyramids, shattering and flying in every direction. The pack on which they were standing quivered and moved dangerously. In several places wide gaps appeared but they were fortunate enough not to fall in.

When the pressure eased, they returned to the place where they had left the Neptune. Instead of a haven of open water they found great masses of ice, twisted and piled in grotesque fashion as though some giant of the north had been playing a game all his own.

"We've seen the last of the Neptune," said Bob Smith sadly. "It was a good tub but not good enough to beat the Arctic."

But Bob was wrong for on the far side of the twisted mass of ice they came upon the bow of the Neptune. From all appearances the shell of the submarine had withstood the terrific pressure and the undersea craft had been hurled out of the water and caught fast in the ice.

It would be impossible to use the Neptune as a means of travel but if the ice held its grip, they could live in the submarine until a rescue expedition could reach them.

Axes were brought from the supplies they had taken off the Neptune and the crew turned to the task of chopping a hole through the ice until they reached the main hatch. Working in shifts, it took them two hours to accomplish the task.

When the hatch was finally opened, Gilbert Mathews insisted that he be the first to enter for the danger of chlorine gas lurked inside the Neptune. If the batteries had upset, the deadly gas might have formed. Anxiously the crew awaited the return of their leader. They cheered wildly when he called that there was no sign of gas and they tumbled back inside for a thorough inspection. Seams had been wrenched so severely that the Neptune would sink like a rock if it ever slid into the ocean but it was dry and comfortable inside and there was plenty of fuel oil in the tanks to keep them warm for months to come.

The first thing was to send word of their plight to the outside world.

The portable radio with its aerial was set up on the ice outside and Harry sat down to send out the first message and ask for relief. The static had cleared since his last attempt and he finally picked up an amateur station at Hopedale, Labrador, to which he communicated the events which had befallen the Neptune. As nearly as possible, Harry gave their position and asked that the officers of the Goliath at Bellevue, Ky., be notified at once.

The operator at Hopedale, after recovering from the astonishment of Harry's message, promised to relay it at once.

The hours dragged by and there was no reply from the operator at Hopedale, except that he had relayed the message to Montreal for further transmission.

The tent which had been erected around Harry's portable set was little protection from the bitter wind and he was numb from cold and miserable when the Hopedale operator finally came back at him. The message had reached Bellevue. The reply was on the way. It cracked through the ether.

"Goliath leaves at midnight. Estimate distance to you is 5,500 miles. Should make it in 60 hours after departure. Signed, Andy High, Assistant Pilot."

Harry ran to the Neptune with the message and the news it contained cheered them greatly. With the wind rapidly whipping into a storm, they took refuge in the warmth of the Neptune and awaited the coming of the Goliath.

CHAPTER XVI
Rescue in the Arctic

For two days after the static cleared, there was no word from the silent northland. Bert, Serge, and Andy remained in the radio room continuously, calling vainly for the Neptune but each time their call went unheeded.

"Something mighty serious has happened to the Neptune," declared Bert, "or Harry would have answered just as soon as the static cleared."

"I'm afraid you're right," said Andy. "They were getting into dangerous water when we last heard from them. Personally, I've doubted all along that the Neptune would ever get to the North Pole. The ice pack there is too solid. They'd have to do too much underwater cruising."

"Do you think they've been trapped under the ice?" asked Bert anxiously.

"No," replied Andy, "for they have the ice drill to cut a path to safety. But a submarine has so many things that can go wrong."

Late the second day Andy's father returned from Washington and they informed him of the gravity of the situation.

"How long would it take to get the Goliath ready for a polar trip?" he asked Andy.

"Not much more than six hours," Andy replied.

"Better warn the crew to stand by. If we don't hear from the Neptune in another 48 hours we'll start north in an attempt to locate them."

Two hours later the Canadian station at Montreal broke in with an urgent message.

"Amateur operator at Hopedale, Labrador, has just messaged that submarine Neptune is disabled and caught in ice. Crew safe. Approximate position: latitude 82° 21′ longitude, east 9° 31′. Ask relief expedition."

Bert copied the message with a hand that shook so much the words were little more than a scrawl.

"Tell Montreal to stand by," said Andy, "while I rush this over to Dad and Captain Harkins." Andy found his father and the commander of the Goliath at the hotel where he burst in on their conference, the message in his hand.

"I was afraid of something like this," said Andy's father. "The navy people in Washington were inclined to be pretty pessimistic when I talked with them, yesterday. Well, what do you say Captain?"

The commander of the Goliath asked Andy for the latest weather report. It was favorable.

"We'll start north at midnight," he said.

"Will you be able to make the trip, Dad?" asked Andy.

"Sorry, son, but I'm due back in Washington tomorrow for a conference that may mean the construction of more ships like the Goliath. The army people have been tremendously pleased with the performance and are anxious for more, semi-commercial, semi-military dirigibles."

Andy hurried back to the radio room where he communicated the news to Bert and Serge. The message that the Goliath would start north at midnight flashed to Montreal but static delayed its transmission to Hopedale, to which it was finally relayed and from there sent on to the waiting crew of the Neptune.

Reporters assigned to Bellevue to cover various trial flights of the Goliath sent out the news of the Neptune's fate and the word that the Goliath was starting north at midnight. Through the early hours of the night the hangar was ablaze with light as final preparations were made.

Every motor was thoroughly checked, extra helium put in the gas cells and every precaution taken to insure the success of the long flight.

Andy and Captain Harkins studied charts of the northland, plotting their proposed course.

It was finally agreed that they would fly north and east to Montreal and then almost due north nearly 3,000 miles along the 76th meridian until they reached Etah, Greenland, on the northwestern tip of that ice-covered land. At Etah they would swing east, skirting the north coast of Greenland, then out over the desolate waste of ice on the last leg of their trip to find the crew of the Neptune.

By eleven-thirty every member of the crew selected for the rescue trip was aboard, including two mail clerks. There would be no transfer of the mail to the Neptune but the postoffice department had rushed a special cancellation from Washington and letters already aboard would be carried into the Arctic. At the scene of the rescue of the Neptune's crew the postal clerks would cancel the letters with the special stamp.

When the Goliath started out of its hangar at midnight on the second of July, there were 62 men aboard, including the two postoffice clerks. The crew had been reduced to a minimum for they would pick up the 31 men from the Neptune.

A typical July heat wave had gripped the nation for three days and they were glad to soar into the cooler heights. A thin moon peeped down at them as the great silver airship climbed into the sky and started north on its mission of rescue.

Lights of Bellevue vanished in the night. They went up to eight thousand feet and headed for Montreal. Bert, in the radio room, advised the Canadian station of their start and asked that the news be sent on to the Neptune, via the station at Hopedale.

Andy made a thorough trip over the Goliath while Serge remained in the control room as first assistant to Captain Harkins. In the last month Serge had proved invaluable. He was thoroughly capable of handling the

Goliath and had the ability to size up an emergency in an instant and make the right decision.

A little more than an hour after leaving Bellevue, the lights of Pittsburgh appeared to their right. Tongues of flame from the steel furnaces along the Monongahela shot into the night as though in greeting to the king of the skyways.

The sky was brightening with the rose of a summer dawn when they passed over Buffalo and headed down Lake Ontario.

Captain Harkins, who had been at the controls, complained of a severe abdominal pain and retired into the main lounge, leaving Andy in charge. As they neared Montreal, the commander's suffering became more intense.

"I'm going to radio ahead and have a doctor meet us at Montreal," said Bert. "Captain Harkins is a mighty sick man and unless I miss my guess, the trouble is acute appendicitis."

Andy agreed and told Serge to make preparations to land the Goliath when they reached the airport outside Montreal. Fortunately there was a mooring mast that had been used by British dirigibles in their trans-Atlantic flights.

It was eight o'clock when the Goliath nosed over Montreal and prepared to descend after its 750 mile flight from its home field. A company from a Canadian regiment stationed in the city had bean turned out and was ready to assist in bringing down the big airship. News that the Goliath would stop had spread over the city and roads leading to the airport were jammed with cars.

With Andy at the main elevator and rudder controls and Serge beside him with a megaphone to direct the actions of the ground crew, they brought the Goliath to an easy landing. As soon as the big ship was fastened securely to the mooring mast Andy hastened back into the main salon where a doctor, who had boarded it the moment they landed, was examining Captain Harkins.

"Acute appendicitis," was the verdict and the doctor added: "To continue on this flight will undoubtedly cost Captain Harkins his life."

"We've got to go on," protested the commander of the Goliath. "The lives of 31 men in the Neptune, trapped in the Arctic, depend on us."

"You've got to think of yourself once in a while," replied the surgeon tartly.

"We can take the Goliath on, Captain Harkins," said Andy. "Serge has demonstrated that he is an expert pilot and navigator. Between the two of us we can handle the ship."

Captain Harkins smiled through pain-tightened lips.

"I'm sure you can," he said, "but you'd better get an official O. K. from your father. He planned to fly back to Washington but you may be able to get him at Bellevue before he starts."

Bert got through to Bellevue at once and in five minutes Andy was talking with his father by radiophone.

"We've got to go on," said the assistant pilot of the Goliath, "and Captain Harkins is desperately ill. Serge and I can take the Goliath through if you'll give your permission."

"Then don't waste any time," replied the executive vice president of the National Airways. "Tell Captain Harkins I'll fly up to see him as soon as possible. Good luck, son, and the best of weather."

Breakfast was served to the crew while the Goliath was moored at the Montreal airport and at nine o'clock Andy gave orders to resume the flight.

Captain Harkins refused to leave the airport until the Goliath was under way and he watched the big ship move away from the mooring mast and soar into the sky from his cot beside an ambulance. Andy dipped the nose of the Goliath in salute to its commander and then headed the dirigible due north, following just east of the 76th meridian.

The day was clear and warm with a slight breeze from the south to speed them on their way and they roared into the northland at a steady hundred miles an hour. The fertile lands around Montreal were replaced by the heavier forests of middle Quebec and as the sun sped on its western path they looked down on a desolate land of brush, swamp and giant mosquitoes which infested the region in summer. There was little habitation in the country below them for it was a quagmire in summer and a frozen waste in winter.

There were innumerable lakes and rivers sighted during the day but by sundown these had thinned out into a few streams which sent their waters westward into Hudson Bay.

Bert kept in almost constant communication with Montreal for the rescue flight of the Goliath was the news of the hour for every paper in the United States and Canada.

Serge had taken a long afternoon shift at the controls while Andy slept and at sundown they changed, Serge going back into the main cabin for a warm supper and a few hours sleep. At midnight he would relieve Andy.

The wind had died down to a whisper. The sky was brilliant with stars and the Goliath made steady progress northward. There was a chill in the air by midnight and Serge had on his sheepskin when he came forward to relieve Andy.

"They're having trouble with No. 5 engine again," said Andy, "and I'm going back and see what's up. I'll have them cut it off until they find out just what's the matter."

Serge nodded, squinted at the chart and compass, and swung the nose of the Goliath one point east.

Back in No. 5 engine room Andy found the motor crew battling a stubborn piece of machinery. The motor would turn over all right but they couldn't get the necessary speed. Andy slipped into a pair of coveralls and worked with the crew. The trouble was in the timing and it took them two hours to do the job.

When Andy returned to the main gondola, the sky was light in the east for they were getting into a latitude where the summer nights were short and the days extremely long. Andy stepped into the control room and Serge pointed ahead of them to a blue expanse of water.

"Hudson Strait," he cried and Andy, hardly believing the words, looked at the chart. An hour later they were cutting across a corner of Fox Land. Then the Goliath was over Baffin Land with the waters of Baffin Bay ahead and to their right.

At five a.m. Andy, who had slept for two hours, relieved Serge. A sharp wind had come out of the north and the Goliath's speed was down to seventy miles an hour.

The broad expanse of Baffin Bay was dotted with ice. They nosed out over Home Bay with the open area of the

South water beneath them. Ahead was the great area of everlasting ice known as the Middle ice. For three hours the Goliath fought its way over the ice sheet. Then came the 25 mile stretch of open water known as Middle water and then another sheet of desolate ice. It was noon when the Goliath finally left the Middle ice and looked down on the berg-dotted stretch of North water. To their right was that majestic land of eternal ice—Greenland, while to their left was the desolate reaches of Ellesmere island.

Serge took over the controls but Andy, instead of going back to rest, remained at the window, looking down at the ever-changing panorama.

Bert had managed to pick up the wireless station at Etah and had asked for a weather report.

"Clear but a thirty mile wind from the north," Etah had replied, when the operator had recovered from his astonishment at learning of the proximity of the Goliath.

With their speed greatly curtailed by the strong wind and a desire to economize as much as possible on fuel, it was late in the day when the Goliath stuck its nose into Smith Sound and looked down at Etah, the farthest north year-round settlement of Greenland.

The Goliath dropped low over Etah in salute to its residents. Then the motors of the Goliath echoed their power through the stillness of the Arctic, Andy brought the nose up, and they proceeded up Smith's Sound and into Kane Basin.

Ahead of them loomed a gray blanket of fog and Andy sent the Goliath climbing for altitude. Four, five, six, even seven thousand feet they fought their way against the bitter wind but the drifting mist of gray enveloped them. They came down to eight hundred feet but there was no escape. The fog clung to the earth and it was impossible to see more than two hundred feet ahead of the control room. Double lookouts were posted and extra men ordered into the observation cockpits atop the Goliath with telephone sets strapped to them so they could communicate any possible danger or send news of a break in the fog bank.

The Goliath crept ahead under reduced speed, barely feeling its way along. Andy knew that below them was the great ice cap which covered Greenland and in the region over which they were now flying an occasional mountain peak reared its head through the eternal blanket of ice and snow. The danger of colliding with such a peak was known to every member of the crew and not a man so much as closed his eyes while the Goliath battled the fog.

The real danger from the fog, which only Andy and Serge realized, was ice. In less than half an hour the outer covering of the Goliath was sheathed in ice. The sides of the gondola were covered with the treacherous stuff and even the windows froze over. It was necessary to lower them and the cold fog swept into the control room. Sheepskins were buttoned close as the Goliath moved slowly ahead.

Serge kept his eyes on the altimeter. The needle was wavering at eight hundred feet. Then it dropped to seven-fifty and finally to seven hundred. The weight of the ice was forcing them down.

Serge nudged Andy and pointed significantly to the needle. It was down to six seventy-five. Andy nodded grimly and ordered more speed, at the same time trying to nose the Goliath higher with the increased lifting power of the additional speed.

They gained a bare hundred feet, held it for five minutes, and then saw the needle of the altimeter start down.

"Take the controls," Andy told Serge. "I'm going to ask for volunteers to go on top with me and try and chop the ice loose."

"You can't do that," protested Serge. "The risk is too great. Someone will slip off and be killed."

"It's either going up top and trying to clear off the ice or wait here until we're forced down and crash into something, which would mean the loss of the Goliath and the end of the rescue flight to the Neptune. I've got to go."

There was no hesitancy among the crew in volunteering for the dangerous task. They equipped themselves with short axes and steel bars, special steel cleated shoes and ropes fastened around their waists. Andy divided his crew of volunteers, four of them going aft and three of them accompanying him aloft at the bow of the Goliath.

When they emerged in the observation cockpit where another member of the crew was huddled trying to peer into the fog, they found themselves in a world alone.

Ahead, behind, and on each side stretched the solid wall of cold, gray mist. The top of the Goliath shone dully under the sheet of ice, the depth of which was increasing every minute.

"Lash yourselves to the steel cable along the catwalk," Andy cautioned them, "and be careful in using the axes. Don't chop through the metalized covering if you can help it."

The men nodded grimly and crept cautiously out on the catwalk, each one careful to fasten the rope around his body. Setting the spikes on their shoes firmly into the ice, they began hacking away at the menacing shield which covered the Goliath.

It was a slow, tedious task and the air was bitter cold. They cleaned off the forward part of the catwalk and then started cautiously out on top of the Goliath. Great sheets of ice slipped away under the prying of their bars but it seemed that new sheets formed almost as fast as they pried the old ones loose.

Andy's hands became numb and his face felt like an icy mask.

The lookout in the observation cockpit shouted at them.

"Control room says we're holding steady now at five hundred feet. Asks if you want more help."

"Tell them to send up a relief crew," replied Andy. Ten minutes later three fresh men were working with him and they attacked the ice with renewed vigor. Andy felt fortunate that there had been no accident so far but the thought was hardly in his mind when one of the new men, overly-enthusiastic, slipped and disappeared in the fog. His safety rope was fastened to the cable along the catwalk, but he had been in too much haste to tie it securely and Andy saw the rope slipping. Somewhere over the side of the Goliath this man was hanging, undoubtedly feeling the quiver of the rope as the knot slipped.

Forgetting his own danger, Andy hurled himself along the catwalk. He seized the other man's safety rope just before the knot gave way. Andy's arms jerked out straight and he cried aloud at the sudden pain. He wrapped his legs around the cable on the catwalk and sprawled out on top of the Goliath, head-foremost toward the edge over which the other man had disappeared.

Andy's cries brought the attention of the watch in the observation cockpit and the other two men working on top with him. As fast as the treacherous condition of the catwalk would permit, they hastened toward him but to Andy their progress was painfully slow.

The rope was slipping through his hands. His fingers tightened until it seemed they would crack but they were so numb from cold he couldn't put his full strength on the rope. It was slipping faster and faster. Somewhere on the other end the man who had been working beside him only a minute before was swinging like a pendulum along the side of the ice-encrusted dirigible.

Andy cried out again. He saw the three coming to his aid hurl themselves toward him. He closed his eyes. The rope was slipping faster. Something hit him so hard that he gasped for breath and the rope raced through his fingers. He clutched at it and his fingers closed against his own palms.

When Andy opened his eyes one of the crew was bending over him while the other two were pulling their companion up over the side of the Goliath. They had reached Andy just as his numbed fingers let go their hold.

A minute later the man who had been looking death in the face was safe on the catwalk, grateful to Andy for the risk he had taken.

Bert, who had sensed something wrong when the watch in the forward cockpit had failed to answer, came charging up. Andy was in no condition to remain up top longer and Bert made him go below into one of the engine rooms to thaw out.

Crews on top of the Goliath were changed every half hour and in this manner the dirigible wallowed through the fog. It was mid-forenoon before the haze showed any signs of lifting but at noon there was a definite break and the Arctic sun soon dispelled the menace in gray.

When Andy was able to shoot their position again, he found that the Goliath was approaching Cape Morris Jessup, the northernmost tip of Greenland.

There were irregular leads in the ice pack which surrounded the cape, but these soon dropped behind and the Goliath moved out over the white expanse of the silent Arctic. They were on the last leg of their long flight, heading east and north now for the position from which Harry had sent his appeal for help. The second day slipped away and they recorded the coming of the third in their log book.

They were fifty-five hours out from Bellevue. The sky was clear but the chill wind still swept out of the north. The interior of the main cabin and control room was warm again and the crew experienced no discomfort in its flight.

They crossed the Greenwich meridian at noon the third day. The Neptune was somewhere east of them by nine degrees and 31 minutes and about two degrees north. Andy altered the course slightly and the Goliath swept nearer the North Pole, although still some three hundred miles from that visionary goal.

Every man who was not on duty in the control or engine rooms was at the windows or stationed in the observation cockpits atop the dirigible, straining ahead for some glimpse of the Neptune and its marooned crew.

Static had been bad all morning but Bert kept up an incessant call for Harry. It was an hour after crossing the Greenwich meridian when he received his first answer and his wild whoop of joy brought Andy into the radio room on the run.

"I'm talking with Harry now," cried Bert. "He says to hurry. The pack ice is breaking up and the Neptune may be lost at any minute."

"Tell them to get out of the tin tub and get onto the ice where they'll be safer," replied Andy. "We'll be there within another hour."

"Two members of the crew are sick," replied Bert.

"Then they'll have to fix up some kind of shelter on the ice," said Andy.

"And Harry says it looks like a norther is coming up," added the radio operator.

"Tell him we're coming at full speed. Have him keep his set going and use your radio compass in guiding us to him."

Bert agreed and Andy hastened back to the control room.

"Bert's just talked with Harry," he told Serge, "and Harry says it looks like a bad storm is brewing. We'll put on full speed and pick them up just as soon as possible."

Word telephoned down from the observation cockpits warned the control room that clouds to the north looked bad. This news added confirmation to that received from Harry and the Goliath raced over the waste of ice and snow at a hundred miles an hour. Every eye was strained ahead to catch some sign of the trapped submarine and its crew.

"The ice is more open here," Andy told Serge. "I wouldn't be surprised if the Neptune has disappeared by the time we reach there. Harry said the ice was getting dangerous and I warned them to get out at once."

"I've had enough of the Arctic right now," said Serge. "The experience with the fog scared me half to death. I thought sure we were going to crash over Greenland and we would if you hadn't gone aloft and kept enough of it chopped off."

"We ought to be near the Neptune now," said Andy, "unless my calculations are way off."

"Want me to start circling from here?" asked Serge.

Before Andy could reply, Bert came from the radio room.

"The Neptune is due north of us," he cried. "Harry sent a flash. Said he caught a glimpse of us with the sun slanting off the silver sides."

Serge swung the rudder over hard and the Goliath, its motors working rhythmically, bored into the heart of the northland. Ahead a solid wall of gray was mounting toward the heavens. In less than an hour the blizzard would be on them.

Five minutes later the watch in the No. 1 cockpit on top phoned that he had sighted the Neptune.

"Crew's on the ice," was the terse message. "The sub's still in sight but the ice is moving and it won't be long until the sub is gone."

Andy's keen eyes were the first in the control room to sight the marooned crew of the Neptune. Behind them he saw the great ridge of ice in which the Neptune had been caught. The dark nose of the undersea craft was still in sight but the ice was heaving and churning under the pressure of the moving ice pack.

Fissures in the ice were widening and the wind swooped out of the north with an ominous roar. Flurries of snow swept past them. The temperature was dropping fast. The rescue must be a matter of minutes or the Arctic might claim the Goliath as well as the Neptune.

"You're better at a landing than I am," Serge told Andy. "Take over."

Andy stepped into the place of command and under his skillful hands the Goliath slid down toward the crew of the Neptune. Steel cables, with heavy grapnels, had been rigged especially for a landing on the ice. When Andy gave the order to shut off the engines, the steel hooks were dropped. They caught on the uneven ice and electric winches to which they were fastened rapidly drew the Goliath down until the main gondola rested just above the ice pack.

Harry was the first to reach the gondola where he was greeted enthusiastically by Andy, Bert and Serge.

"You're just in time," he told them. "The ice is breaking up. That means the end of the Neptune and this blizzard would probably have finished us."

While Harry was talking, the sound of the coming storm was drowned by a series of splintering crashes. The ice ahead of them heaved and buckled.

Great chunks were hurled into the air. The nose of the Neptune was pushed straight up. For a moment the submarine hung in this position. Then, to the accompaniment of the steady booming of the ice, the sleek, steel hull slid from view. It was gone in ten seconds—devoured by the ever-hungry Arctic.

Gilbert Mathews, who had aged years in the last few days, stumbled across the ice.

"Thank heaven you've arrived," he cried. "We must hurry. The blizzard is almost upon us."

In twos and threes the crew of the Neptune hurried toward the Goliath. A twilight had settled over the scene and the lights from the cabin windows of the Goliath shone strangely through the dusk of the coming storm.

Serge and a crew from the Goliath brought the two men from the Neptune who were ill aboard. Some of them carried a few personal possessions. Most of them had only the clothes they wore but they were thankful to have even those.

The last hours aboard the Neptune had been hours of terror with the constant danger of the ice breaking up and dropping them into the depths of the Arctic. With rescue at hand, some of them were almost hysterical with joy. Mathews spoke to Andy.

"I know the Arctic," he said. "Get out of here as soon as you can. This storm is going to be terrific. As soon as the last man is aboard, take off."

Every motor was running smoothly and easily.

"Stand by for a quick take off and a run before the storm," he warned the engineers. "Our lives will depend on you. We've got to make time."

Back in one of the cabins the postal clerks were busy cancelling the letters which had been the only pay cargo aboard the Goliath on the polar trip. They were obvious to the dangers of the coming storm and Andy envied them their lack of worry.

"Everybody on," reported Serge. "Let's go."

"Let's go," echoed Andy and the command was flashed back to the engine rooms. The Goliath quivered to the pulsation of the powerful motors. To save time, the steel cables with the grapnels were dropped on the ice and the Goliath shook its nose at the gathering storm as it roared aloft.

The take-off had not come a moment too soon. The Goliath had barely turned around and headed south, when the blizzard struck in all its fury. A dry, biting snow enveloped the dirigible and the lights from the cabin windows made only faint glows in the sea of swirling white.

With motors turning over at full speed, the Goliath raced due south. But fast though the Goliath traveled, the storm kept pace. Andy was thankful for one thing. The snow was dry. It wouldn't freeze to the sides and force them down.

The air outside was bitter cold and despite the heating system in the gondola, a penetrating chill crept in.

"How about the two men who are sick?" Andy asked the explorer.

"It's flu," replied Mathews. "They're over the worst of it but so weak they can hardly move. However, if they had been exposed to many hardships, it would have turned into pneumonia and they wouldn't have had a chance."

Bert had managed to send out a flash on the rescue of the crew of the Neptune and had added that they were running before an Arctic blizzard. This meager information was relayed by the Hopedale station and for hours a waiting world wondered and waited for news of the Goliath and its daring crew. They knew the king of the skies was battling for its life somewhere in the northland; they knew that its commander was ill in a Montreal hospital and they wondered at the stuff of which Andy and his assistants were made. Could they bring the Goliath through the dangers and rigors of a blizzard in the Arctic?

Radio stations all over the northland tuned their sensitive ears for some word from the Goliath, but the wall of static had dropped and their calls went unanswered.

In the meantime, the Goliath was racing south, its motors on full as it sped through the storm. They were doing a hundred and thirty miles an hour but the snow stayed with them and the cold was even more intense.

The great ship was running blind. The only direction was south. Anything to escape the tearing savagery of the Arctic. Serge stood silent at the controls while Andy went on a tour of inspection. The engine crews were getting drowsy from their long vigil and he ordered the steward to serve a hot lunch for everyone.

Andy was in the rear of the Goliath, leaving the last engine room, when he heard a peculiar whistling sound. A draft of cold air struck him and he turned quickly toward the tail of the ship, stopping only long enough to get a flashlight from the engine room. He worked his way along the narrow catwalk in the tail. The blast of air was stronger. The beam of his flashlight traced a finger of light through the duralumin girders and cables which formed and controlled the main elevator.

The light fastened on one section of the right elevator. There was a great tear in the metalized fabric through which the wind was whistling in an increasing crescendo. Unless the tear was repaired at once, the Goliath would be in grave danger of getting out of control for the opening was growing larger and would soon render the elevators useless.

Andy ran back to the engine room where he telephoned Serge to reduce their speed to a minimum. The same call brought Bert and Harry back on the run and another call brought two expert riggers with a roll of the metal cloth and a can of cement, which they heated in the engine room.

The chief rigger, Mac Glassgow, looked at the rip in the elevator.

"It's a mean one to fix," he asserted, "but we'll do the job."

"We've got to," urged Andy. "It's growing larger every minute."

"An inside job won't be so hard," said Mac, "but to make it stick, it should be patched from the outside."

"There's no place to land and do that," protested Bert.

"I know, I know," said Mac, "but an inside patch will never hold."

"You mean someone ought to go up top, lower themselves down on the outside, and make the patch?" asked Andy.

Mac nodded.

"That's the ticket," he said. "I'm a bit too old and stiff or I'd do it in a minute. The Graf Zeppelin's crew had to do it one time off the Atlantic coast in weather about as bad as this."

"I'll go up," replied Andy. "Get the patch ready, Mac. Bert and Harry will come along to lower me away."

Andy's friends protested that it was a foolhardy attempt, but he refused to listen to them.

"We are all in grave danger," he said. "The attempt must be made. As long as you fellows hang onto the rope I'll be in no danger."

Other members of the crew were summoned and under Mac's expert direction a temporary patch was placed inside the elevator fin. While this was being accomplished, Andy prepared for the outside job.

A harness of leather straps was rigged around his shoulders and body and to this was attached a strong new one inch rope. Mac had cut the patch to the proper size and the cement had been placed in a double bucket to retain its heat. The motors were turning over just fast enough to give the Goliath steerage way.

Andy and his two companions ascended the ladder to the rear right cockpit, from which the commander of the Goliath was to be lowered over the side.

The wind was blowing a gale that chilled them instantly.

"You'll freeze to death before you get down to the fin," said Bert.

"I'll hug this cement pot," replied Andy. "All set?"

Andy slid over the side and Bert and Harry lowered away on the rope. Foot by foot Andy eased down over the smooth side of the Goliath. Twenty, thirty, forty feet he went out and down. Just below he caught the glow of light inside the fin and the outline of the makeshift patch which Mac and his rigger had slapped on inside.

The young pilot sprawled flat on the surface of the fin, arms outstretched. The cloth to complete the patch was fastened on his back.

With chilled hands he opened the top of the cement pot and seized the brush. The rip in the fin was about twelve feet long and two feet wide. Andy slapped the cement on the back end first, shut the top of the pot, readied for the patch, and put the end in place before the cement had a chance to cool. The Goliath was drifting through the storm and Andy had patched the end of the hole which received the greatest force of the wind.

He worked forward carefully, stopping now to apply the cement liberally, then unrolling the patch, and moving ahead another foot to repeat the operation. In the fin beneath, he could hear Mac, the rigger, shouting encouragement. He needed it. He was worn almost to the breaking point by the responsibility which had been on his shoulders ever since the Goliath left the airport at Montreal. Tears froze to his cheeks and he cried aloud at the pain in his cold white hands. His movements were mechanical. Slap on the cement, unroll the patch, slap on the cement, unroll the patch.

Suddenly there was no more cement to put on, no more cloth to unroll. The job was done. The danger that the fin might be ripped off by the wind was over. Andy closed his eyes and his numbed hands slipped. There was a sensation of falling and he knew that he was slipping off the fin but he was in a lethargy, unable to help himself. He felt himself dip over the edge of the fin; knew he was falling into the storm and darkness.

When he opened his eyes half an hour later he was in the warmth of one of the rear engine rooms. Bert and Harry were beside him.

"What happened while I was on the fin?" demanded Andy.

"The cold got you," replied Bert, "and you slipped off. Good thing we had a rope around you."

"Is the fin all right?" Andy asked eagerly.

Mac Glassgow, the chief rigger who had remained in the background, stepped up.

"Best job of patching I ever saw," he exclaimed. "We'll have no more trouble with that fin this trip."

"How's the storm?" was Andy's next question.

"We're running out of it now," replied Harry.

"Serge just phoned back that the sky was clearing and it is much warmer."

Despite Andy's protest, they made him go to bed, and Harry sat down to see that their wishes were enforced.

When Andy awoke again the sky had cleared and the Goliath was cruising through brilliant sunshine. The events of the storm were like a nightmare.

Serge was still at the controls. He was tired and worn by the long ordeal, but he smiled happily when he saw Andy.

Bert came out of the radio room with a sheaf of messages.

"I've sent out a complete story of our trip," he informed Andy, "and messages are coming in almost every minute now. Here's a couple you'll want." The first was from Andy's father, then in Washington.

"Have just learned of fine work of yourself and crew of Goliath. I'm proud of you, son."

The other was from Captain Harkins. It read: "Great work, Andy. My congratulations to Bert, Harry and Serge. Many happy landings." Andy passed the messages along to Harry and Serge, who read them eagerly.

"You've done a fine piece of work in taking the Goliath into the Arctic and bringing back the Neptune's crew," said Harry. "You deserve all the congratulations."

"They're embarrassing," grinned Andy, "for you fellows deserve just as much credit as I do."

"We won't quarrel over that," said Serge. "Incidentally, if anyone is curious, that point of land to our left is Cape Bismark and that rather inhospitable-looking stretch of ice and snow beyond is King William land."

"Which means nothing at all to me," replied Bert.

"If you could read a chart," replied Serge lightly, "you'd know that we are now off the east coast of Greenland, proceeding south by west at ninety miles an hour with clear skies and a favoring tail wind. Also, I'm going to bed."

With motors tuned perfectly to their task, the Goliath sped southward toward New York, where it would stop to land the crew of the Neptune. Andy, again at the controls, smiled happily for the Goliath had proved beyond any question that it was master of the elements—king of the skies.

SECRET FLIGHT

The exciting sequel to *Air Monster*
By Edwin Green

Back from their victorious battle with an Arctic storm and the rescue of the crew of the submarine Neptune, Andy High and his companions, Bert Benson, Harry Curtis, and Serge Latko, find themselves plunged into a series of adventures that dwarfs anything they have encountered in their Arctic exploits.

The Goliath, largest and mightiest dirigible in the world, is scarcely broken in for its transcontinental service when orders from the navy department, which helped the National Airways finance the big ship, send the Goliath away, speeding to a secret rendezvous of the Pacific fleet.

A new revolt has stirred Russia and, with the recent large gold strikes in Alaska, that territory looks highly desirable to the new regime in Russia. Large concentrations of Russians have been reported in Siberia and an international crisis, which might embroil the entire world, looms in the Pacific. The entire strength of the American navy is concentrated in the Pacific, ready for any emergency.

Because of his knowledge of secret police duties, Serge, former member of the Rubanian secret service, is assigned the dangerous task of entering Siberia and learning the exact plans of the Russians. It is the task of Andy High and the Goliath to land Serge safely in Russian territory and return him to the fleet when he has completed his mission. The Goliath, winging its way through the high heavens to avoid detection, takes Serge to Siberia where he learns that another world conflict is in the making.

How the daring band of young Americans in the Goliath thwart the plans of the Russians brings this story of modern intrigue to a powerful climax that will thrill every young reader.